Return to the Rain

Return to the Rain

— *Dreaming of Home* —

a Novel

LINDA L. GRAHAM

LUMINARE PRESS
WWW.LUMINAREPRESS.COM

Return to the Rain: Dreaming of Home
Copyright © 2024 by Linda L. Graham

All rights reserved. This book or any portion thereof may not be reproduced or used in any manner whatsoever without the express written permission of the publisher, except for the use of brief quotations in a book review.

Printed in the United States of America

Luminare Press
442 Charnelton St.
Eugene, OR 97401
www.luminarepress.com

LCCN: 2024919639
ISBN: 979-8-88679-691-9

With love to Raul

You are always there for me.

Contents

Part 1
THE NORTHWEST:

Prologue 3

Chapter 1 7
Chapter 2 15

Part 2
MEXICO

Chapter 3 21
Chapter 4 26
Chapter 5 29
Chapter 6 35
Chapter 7 38
Chapter 8 42
Chapter 9 44
Chapter 10 47
Chapter 11 53
Chapter 12 57
Chapter 13 59
Chapter 14 62
Chapter 15 66
Chapter 16 69
Chapter 17 72
Chapter 18 75
Chapter 19 78
Chapter 20 79
Chapter 21 82
Chapter 22 86
Chapter 23 91

Chapter 24 95
Chapter 25 98
Chapter 26 103
Chapter 27 109
Chapter 28 111

Part 3
THE NORTHWEST:

Chapter 29 115
Chapter 30 119
Chapter 31 122
Chapter 32 126
Chapter 33 129
Chapter 34 132
Chapter 35 135
Chapter 36 137
Chapter 37 142
Chapter 38 144
Chapter 39 148
Chapter 40 151
Chapter 41 153
Chapter 42 155
Chapter 43 158
Chapter 44 160
Chapter 45 164
Chapter 46 166
Chapter 47 168
Chapter 48 171
Chapter 49 174
Chapter 50 176
Chapter 51 179
Chapter 52 182

Epilogue 185

This book is a work of fiction. Names, characters, businesses, organizations, places, events, and incidents either are the product of the author's imagination or are used fictitiously. Any resemblance to actual persons, living or dead, events, or locales is entirely coincidental.

Also by Linda L. Graham

INDIANA SUMMER:
From Cornfields and Lightning Bugs
A Memoir

TWO MICE AND A DRAGONFLY:
How Cats Help a Disconnected Family
A Novel

FLY HOME, BUTTERFLY:
In Search of a Father
A Novel

Characters

Casandra (Cassie)

Luis Mendez—Cassie's husband

Abbie –Cassie and Luis' daughter

Tully McMillen—Cassie's adopted mother

Sebastian and Mandy—Tully's cats

Jasmine—Cassie's adopted sister

John—Jasmine's husband

Josh and Josie—Jasmine and John's children

Robert Harris—Cassie's biological father

Luke—Cassie's uncle

Amy and Thomas—Luke's wife and child

Ray and Vicki—Cassie's grandparents

Claire, Preston, and Tommy—Cassie's friends

Jose—tour guide, Cassie's biological brother

Marie, Esteban, Viviana, and Mercedes—Luis' family

Bogey—Robert's dog and Destiny—horse from stable.

Sharon—Cassie's editor

Geraldo—waiter

Jake—Viviana's baby

Dr. Casey—Cassie's doctor

Sadie—babysitter

Baby Amalia—Cassie's baby

Domino—Cassie's cat

U.S. and Mexico Map

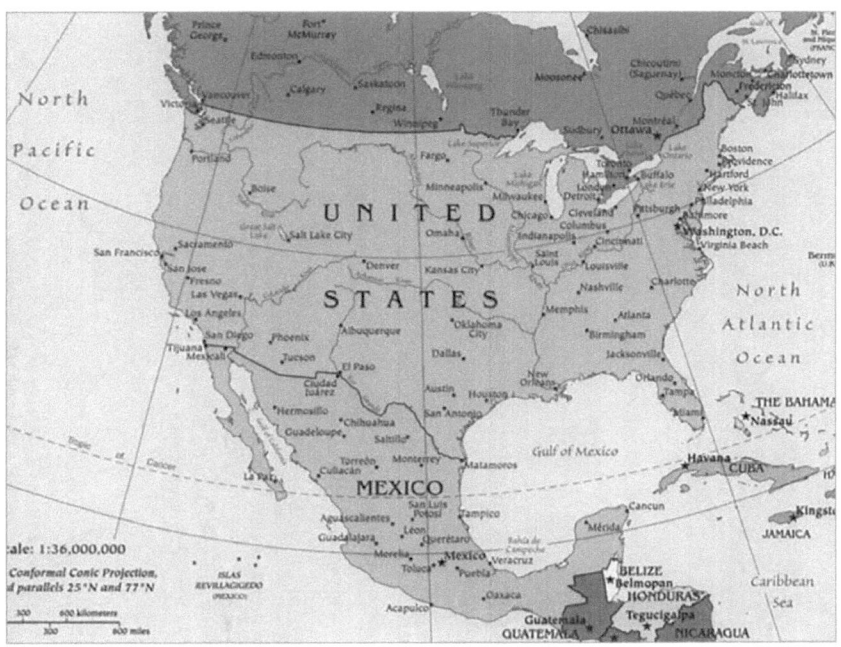

(North America-PICRYL Public Domain Image)

PART 1

The Northwest:

OREGON/WASHINGTON

Prologue

CASSIE

SUMMER 2021

I observed little four-year-old Abigail, or Abbie, as Luis and I referred to her as she scampered from the bottom of the slide and back to the ladder. "Mommy, look! I can slide with no hands!" I heard her delighted laughter as she slid down one more time, this time without touching the sides of the slide.

"Yes! I see you!" I grinned, enjoying the carefree antics of my daughter, grateful for the reprieve from the worry about the restrictions imposed by the Pandemic, now into its second year.

We thought everything would be better by now, but a variant of the virus popped up, crippling the world once more.

I had driven to Springville, Washington from our home in Lincoln City, Oregon. I was anxious to see my family after many months of staying home and not seeing family or friends. We were celebrating Abbie's fourth birthday today, August 25.

"While Abbie plays on the slide and swing, I'll get out the picnic lunch," Tully said, chuckling as she too, watched Abbie. Tully McMillen, my adoptive mother, had joined us outdoors, since it was a safe way to enjoy one another's company without wearing a mask. "I just got a text from Jasmine and she and the kids will be here in five minutes."

"Okay, Mom. I'll just sit here and keep an eye on Abbie," I assured her. Out of the corner of my eye I saw two children running towards the swings and slide. Following at a slow amble was Jasmine, arms full of food and supplies for the picnic. Jasmine was Tully's biological daughter, but I knew Mom loved us both the same.

"They're here!" Abbie exclaimed joyfully, still dashing from the bottom of the slide back to the top. "Josh, Josie, watch me! No hands!" Down she slid one more time, arms raised high to demonstrate.

"Good job, Abbie," ten-year-old Josh replied, acting the older, wiser cousin. He joined her on the slide as did eight-year-old Josie, who grinned excitedly as she mounted the ladder to the slide. I continued to watch my daughter, her short and tightly curled black hair impervious to the wind. The other two children had blonde hair like Jasmine's which whipped around their smiling faces as they slid down by turns, each of them raising their arms.

"Hey, Sis. How are you doing these days?" Jasmine set down her zippered ice chest on the picnic table, and then gave her mother, Tully, a hug. Both Jasmine and Tully immediately began setting out plates, sandwiches, chips, and cupcakes.

"Oh, same as before. Mostly staying at home with Abbie and doing my job online at home. Pretty boring most days but staying well. Can't complain."

"I know what you mean. All of us teachers are so tired of trying to teach online to children instead of in person. The district says we will go to in person learning this fall. I hope so. I want to get back to teaching music instead of regular elementary classroom teaching on a computer." Jasmine said the last word in disgust. "John is sick of it too." John is Jasmine's husband, also a teacher, but in middle school grades.

"Cassie, want to round up the kids and bring them to the table? I brought sanitizing wipes for their hands," Tully asked, pulling out the package from her bag of supplies.

"Sure. Here's some fruit to go with the rest of the lunch." I handed over a large baggie full of sliced red apples, and then walked closer to the playground to get the children.

"Watch this, Aunt Cassie!" Josie chortled. "We can make a train!" Just at that moment, the three of them slid down together, hanging onto one another in a single file, Abbie in the lead. At the bottom, Josh and Josie landed in a heap on top of her. As I ran over to rescue Abbie from the scrambled pile, the three of them burst out laughing.

"Let's do it again!" Abbie cried, untangling herself from the other two.

"Not now. Grandma said it's time to eat. Come on, kids, let's go." I grabbed Abbie's hand and nearly had to drag her away from the other two. Josh and Josie reluctantly trailed behind me.

While we all ate and chatted at the picnic table, my mind drifted back to how I got to this point of having a daughter in the first place. Here I was, at thirty-seven, and my younger sister Jasmine, thirty-three, had a ten-year-old and an eight-year-old. I saw the contented smile on our mom's face as she served up the lunch. We were her life; my adoptive father died from a heart attack while I was still a teenager. I left home at eighteen to search for my biological mother. After I found her, living in a run-down trailer home in Montana, it only raised more questions as to what my biological father was like. Whereas my appearance was obviously African American, my birth mother was not. I lived happily enough with my adopted family; however, I had a deep yearning to discover my identity by finding my real father. I assumed he would look more like me. I spent two years searching for him, going to remote areas of the U.S. in Texas and Mexico.

When I found Robert Harris on a mountain top in Mexico, living in a cabin as a recluse, researching the migration of the

Monarch butterflies as an entomologist, he coldly rejected me. I left, determined to never let him hurt me again.

That was before he showed up unannounced at my wedding in 2012. I was marrying Luis Mendez in Puebla, Mexico. There, just thirty minutes before my wedding was to begin, my father begged for forgiveness and permission to escort me down the aisle.

From that point on, my father and I stayed in touch, and in 2017, my father visited Luis and me. We shared the news with him that we were expecting our daughter later that year. Robert returned after Abbie was born, and we enjoyed Thanksgiving with him for the first time ever at Tully's. That's when a curious twist of fate occurred.

Chapter 1

CASSIE

THANKSGIVING 2017

The overnight bags were packed, waiting at the front door. "Ready everyone?" Luis said brightly, still trying to overcome the silences that seemed to crop up every few minutes.

Robert, or Bob, as he liked to be called, glanced over to Luis, smiling just a little. "As ready as I will ever be." He sighed. "Let's do this!"

My father, Robert Harris, had stayed with Luis and me at our Lincoln City, Oregon beach home in June. It was like a strange and surreal dream. His arrival gave us all an opportunity to get to know one another—our likes, dislikes, and idiosyncrasies, which were many in his case. Luis and I took him sightseeing, driving south to Depoe Bay, where at times, whales can be seen. We never saw one, but the landscape was breath taking. We returned in the evenings to prepare simple foods, usually grilling fish on the barbeque. Afterward, we sat on deck chairs, staring at the waves, attempting conversation. My dad and I had gaps of many years to go over. Sometimes, the silences were awkward, but Luis made an effort to fill in the void. "So, uh, Mr. Harris, do you own the cabin up on the mountain in Mexico?"

"Please, call me Bob. Unfortunately, no. It is on loan to me from the Mexican government. I can keep it only for as long as I continue to document my research on the Monarchs. I love it there. So peaceful." Robert took a sip off his iced tea, staring out again at the high tide which seemed to sneak up closer to our house minute by minute.

That was in June. Now, November 23, my father is back, and it is time to prepare to travel to Springville, Washington, where my mother, Tully McMillen, is hosting Thanksgiving. The whole family will be there, including Jasmine and her husband John, as well as their children, Josh and Josie. Uncle Luke, his wife, Amy, and stepson, Thomas, will be there, along with my grandparents. It will be an imposing group for my father to encounter, although at least, he had already met my mother and sister at our wedding.

We solved one potential problem ahead of time by booking two hotel rooms near to Tully's home in Springville. She had only one spare bedroom, and we didn't want to have a discussion of who slept where. The rest of the family lived in Springville, so of course, it would be easy for them to just show up for the day.

We secured Abbie into her infant seat in the back, where I also sat, with Luis driving and Dad in the front passenger seat. The drive took around five hours, but we had to stop for lunch and bathroom breaks. In all, six hours later we rounded the corner to Tully's condo. I took a deep breath, not knowing how all this would go with the whole family there. Robert wasn't an easy conversationalist; I assumed it was from his scientist background and years of living as a recluse on a mountaintop. During the off season of the migration, he told us that weeks would go by without seeing another human. Fortunately, once a month or every other month, the tour guide, Jose, brought Robert food and supplies that he needed. Sometimes Jose was Robert's only human contact for the nine months or so during the off season. The migration brought tourists there mostly in February through April.

I smiled nervously as I stated the obvious, "Well, here we are!" Luis pulled into an empty parking spot, and we all tumbled out, glad to stretch. While I fumbled with the buckles on Abbie's infant seat, she cried impatiently.

"Hang on. Let me get your seat unbuckled, little one. We're here to see Grandma!" I tried at brightness, hoping to cover the stoic looks of Robert and Luis, who both felt a bit uncomfortable at the prospect of encountering my family. The two men grabbed the luggage while I picked up Abbie, seat and all, and we trudged down the sidewalk and up the stairs to Mom's second story condo. Before we could ring the doorbell, however, the door swung open, and there was Tully, her auburn hair all askance and tied back in a ponytail. I could smell the aromas of roasted turkey and mashed potatoes.

"You're here! Welcome! Jasmine, they're here! And where is my grandbaby?"

"Yes, I heard you. Give me a moment to dry my hands." Before Jasmine appeared, Tully had grabbed each of us in an embrace, awkwardly including Robert, who disentangled himself promptly. She peered into Abie's little face, touching her cheek fondly. "Give her to me!" Tully exclaimed, anxious to hold Abbie.

"Yay! She's here!" Josie cried out; I heard two sets of footsteps, both Josie's and Josh's, running quickly to see baby Abbie. "Oh, so cute!" four-year-old Josie exclaimed, tossing her doll on the floor to take a better look at a real baby.

"Yes, she is," Josh admitted, smiling in spite of himself, two years older than Josie.

Jasmine had also appeared in the doorway to see the baby. "Oh, when I can, Auntie Jasmine must hold her."

"Me first! Come in, come in," Tully commanded. "Hang your coats on the rack and make yourself comfortable. Care for a glass of wine?"

"Uh, yes, please. Mom, I can get what everyone wants. You just continue with what you were doing."

"John went out for some napkins. We forgot to buy those." Jasmine went back to the kitchen to keep chopping vegetables for a relish plate. The kids went off to the spare bedroom to play, and the rest of us were left to carry on trivial conversation. I set Abbie down in the living room in her seat after Tully and Jasmine took turns holding her for a few minutes. I found wine glasses on the counter next to both red and white wine bottles and began serving. Robert and Luis took a glass and settled on opposite ends of the sofa.

"So, when is Uncle Luke arriving? And Grandpa and Grandma?" I asked, trying to keep up a banter from the living room while Tully and Jasmine labored in the kitchen.

"Oh, they called and will be here within thirty minutes or so. No worry." Tully called out from the kitchen, checking on the potatoes with her fork to see if they were ready to mash. Suddenly, Robert rose from his seat and strode into the kitchen.

"May I assist you with the preparation, or carve the turkey when it's time?" He smiled warmly at Tully, looking her over from her frazzled hair to her bright orange apron.

"Oh! Okay, how about you do the carving? I would love for you to take that over," she said, her lustrous blue eyes widening in pleasure.

"Very well," he answered in his low sonorous voice, still standing in the kitchen, as if awaiting another job to do. He took a sip of his red wine, just observing Tully at work. "What else can I do until the carving time?" I noted the exchange from a distance from the living room, wondering where all this would lead, if anywhere. This wasn't like my father at all. He was always so reserved; so calculated. Jasmine signaled me with her eyes, also bewildered at his sudden outgoing behavior. Then, I realized that perhaps, he was, above all else, a gentleman.

"Well, uh, you could get out the plates and carry them to the table if you wish," Mom offered.

"Certainly. Could you point me to the bathroom so I can wash my hands first?" Tully directed him down the hall to the bathroom, and then resumed her work in the kitchen.

"My, such a gentleman!" Tully commented quietly, smiling slightly, humming a little as she mashed the potatoes.

"Yes, he is," Jasmine agreed. I just sat there, mute, taking it all in, not sure what to make of this if anything.

Just as I was about to comment too, the door opened, and John marched in with a grocery bag. "Hey, everyone. Welcome and happy Thanksgiving," he said, not breaking stride as he took his bag to the kitchen. John was the tall, dark, and handsome type, setting down the bag and giving Jasmine a peck on her cheek. He had to bend quite a way down since she was much shorter. "It's crazy out there. You would think no one planned food for their get together until today. Long lines at the checkout."

"John, come greet our guests," Tully said, dropping her potato masher and leading him by the hand into the living room. Robert followed them back into the living room for the formal greeting, a bemused expression on his face. Before Tully could get through the introductions, there was a knock on the door. John dashed over to open it; Uncle Luke, Tully's brother, strode in with his wife, Amy, and stepson, Thomas.

"Mom and Dad are just pulling up; they will be here directly," Uncle Luke stated, carrying two pies into the kitchen. I caught a glimpse of Robert, his eyebrows arching in surprise as he watched Luke from a distance. Luke had retired from his C.I.A. work many years ago, but still carried himself in military stiffness, with his long silver hair tied back in a man-style ponytail. My breath always caught when I saw him; I gave him a grin of mutual understanding. He merely nodded, acknowledging me. We were both wanderers in our former lives. He had disappeared from us for over twenty years, suddenly showing up on Tully's doorstep. From then on, he became a part of our family once again. His wife, Amy, seemed to adore him. She was quiet, unassuming. Thomas must be about eighteen now. He and Luke both towered over Amy.

Just at that moment, we heard slow steps approaching the front door. Luke opened the door, and my grandpa, Ray, and grandma, Vicki appeared. They too, carried in a plate each, and set them on the counter. Tully hugged everyone in turn, and then announced, "Cassie, will you introduce your father and husband, and baby to everyone?"

I hadn't anticipated that but complied. Tully then gave the prayer of thanks and instructed us all in how to go through the food line buffet style.

During the meal, everyone kept quizzing my father about his research in the butterfly sanctuary. Luke sat erect and unmoving, as did Robert, and conversation seemed a bit strained. We made it to dessert, an assortment of pies, including pumpkin and apple, all arranged on the counter. Everyone chose what they wanted and returned to the living room. Tully jumped up to refill coffee cups, and I observed Robert follow her into the kitchen. "Uh, Tully," I overheard him say softly, "would you like to meet me at the hotel lounge for a nightcap later?"

I could hear Mom gasp in surprise, but her eyes held him in a smile. I was shocked as well but concealed my feelings by taking another sip of coffee. "Why, I think I can arrange that," she answered, grinning flirtatiously.

"How about around eight? Will your guests mind?" As he spoke, he picked up dirty plates and began loading them into the dishwasher. Both moved around in the kitchen, gathering plates and putting leftover food into the refrigerator. I looked on in amazement. *What was going on here?* My mouth opened to say as much, but I managed to snap it shut and remained silent. I kept asking myself how my adopted mom and my biological father could possibly be hitting it off. *This can't be happening*, I told myself. I gazed around the room, but no one else seemed to notice. All were engaged in either eating pie or chatting about something. Maybe I was reading too much into it. After all, my father did seem to be a gentleman. Maybe it was just part of his persona to take an interest in the hostess of our gathering.

My mind reverted back to listening in on their conversation. "Oh, I'm pretty certain they will leave for home before then, so that will be good," Tully was saying to Robert.

"Good. Then it's settled,' Robert said, giving my mom a satisfied smile, returning to placing dishes in the dishwasher.

I got up from my seat and began collecting plates and cups from everyone as they finished eating. Anxious, I took them into the kitchen to see just what was really going on between my mom and Robert. It appeared that I had interrupted something; both acted nervous, and put their heads down, working feverishly to get everything put away. Neither said anything more. *Ha!* I thought to myself. *Guess I took care of any further nonsense going on in here.*

Conversation in the living room waned in there as well. Soon, the men drifted off into naps, mouths open, heads crooked to the side. After another hour or so, Uncle Luke and his family left, as well as my grandparents. The day was over; we eventually said our goodbyes and returned to our hotel. At least, Thanksgiving got our introductions of Luis, Robert, and Abbie to the family out of the way. We drove back to Lincoln City the next day, exhausted.

Rain
(Fall)

The clouds release their contents,
Dark, menacing, and threatening, as they pelt down.
Drops of moisture onto the parched ground,
Longing to quench its thirst,
To revitalize green shoots once more,
after the long drought of summer.

Once considered ominous, now the hush
of mists descends upon the city,
A comfort to withered grasses and trees, who reach
up to slake their yearning, though warm weather
buffs mourn the inevitable torrents.
For nature, however, a welcome sign of life restored.
The sun hides its face as the days become shorter.
We huddle indoors, listening to the patter
on leaves and roof tops.
As the dreary days commence.

Linda L. Graham

Chapter 2

Cassie

February 2020

"Cassie, you might want to get down here as soon as you can arrange it," my father said, calling me from Angangueo. Robert had made one of his infrequent trips from his mountain top cabin into the village to purchase supplies himself instead of relying on Jose, the tour guide. "The butterflies are so profuse and are early this year. Very unusual!" I detected excitement in his voice, so rare with him.

"Wow! Dad! I would love to. Maybe I can work it out. I have to ask Tully if she will watch Abbie. Plus, Luis and I will need to arrange time off."

"It would be worth it if you can manage. I have never seen this many at one time in all the years I've lived up here on the biosphere mountain."

I thought it all sounded so difficult, so dubious to figure it all out. But it was worth a try, I quickly decided. Robert knew I had wished to return there but was waiting for Abbie to get a little older to leave her in Tully's care. "I'll see what Mom and Luis have to say. I may call my friends, Claire, Preston, and Tommy as well. I know they would love to see it again. They accompanied me on my excursions looking for you." I chuckled, trying to make light of the all-out effort into finding my dad.

"Right, right. I remember you telling me. So, let me know. And how is Tully, by the way?"

"What? Oh. She's fine," I answered, perplexed at his sudden interest in my mom. Or perhaps not so sudden. I recalled at that moment how Robert had acted so debonair around Mom when we went to her place for Thanksgiving in 2017. Abbie was just a newborn infant at the time.

"Is she enjoying being a grandma?" he persisted, and I was drawn back to our phone conversation.

"Uh, yes, sure. Right. She takes care of Abbie occasionally, but we don't live in the same state, you know. Sometimes I go to Springville to visit her and the family, and she loves it when Abbie is in town. She doesn't seem to care if I'm there or not. It's all about Abbie."

Robert chuckled. "Of course. Typical I would think. Glad she is enjoying." Robert paused, then added, "Give her my regards, will you?"

"Okay. Sure. I'll tell her you said hello." I supposed that's what he meant. So formal and unlike the way I would talk.

"And how is little Abbie?" he asked, almost like an afterthought.

"Oh, she is learning new things every day, and growing so fast. Wish you could see her."

"Yes, me too. It's not easy to get up there. Bring pictures when you come." Robert paused. "So, let me know if you are coming and when. Just leave word with Jose and he will relay to me on his next tour up the mountain."

"Sure, Dad. I wish you had cell phone reception up at the top. So much easier."

"I know. I wish so too, but it's off the grid up there. Just let Jose know the details. We'll figure it out when you get here."

After we hung up, I thought about the possibility of returning to the butterfly sanctuary. I just had to go! However, I was a little perplexed at Robert's interest in Tully after all this time since he saw her last. Maybe it was just a polite intrigue; she represented my adopted family that he in only recent years was aware of.

PART 2

Mexico

Chapter 3

CASSIE

MARCH 2020

The plane set down with a jolt; I reached for the armrests and clung on tightly. We had arrived in Mexico City. The Monarch Butterfly Sanctuary was just a few hours away by bus. I turned my head to grin at Luis, who was also gripping the armrests as the plane slowed down on the tarmac. "Here we are, Cassie. I'm back home in Mexico! I have missed it here. But you and Abbie are so worth living in the U.S." Luis looked at me fondly, putting his arm around my shoulder.

"Are you sure about that?" I teased, leaning onto his shoulder.

"Absolutely. I will be glad to see my family, though, after we leave the sanctuary. But let's just enjoy each moment here. First, on to the butterfly sanctuary!" The plane came to a halt, and we reached up for our carryon luggage.

Our destination by bus was to the state of Michoacan, in the village of Angangueo. Robert's cabin was perched on the mountain peak above, in the heart of the Monarch sanctuary. When I first began my search for Robert in Mexico, I went to the village of Ocampo, where I reached the conclusion that he was not there. We finally got a tip from the university in Monterey, where my father studied, that he had gone to the area of

Angangueo. My mind reverted to all the past searches for him as we rode in the tour bus to Angangueo. I never gave up. The search ended here, but I was totally unprepared for my father's cold rejection once I located him. All of that was in the past now, I reminded myself.

Luis and I had booked a room in the historic-looking hotel in the village. As we disembarked, I glanced around, remembering the first time I was here. Nothing had changed in the years since. The locals were used to the bus unloading tourists. They only gave a cursory glance as we stepped out. There were about six of us. Claire, Preston, and Tommy would be arriving here tomorrow. Our hotel, an ancient crumbling stucco three story structure, was still covered in ivy. Somehow, it looked inviting. After all, this is the village near where I found my father all those years ago. Now, he awaited our visit to the mountaintop. We would ascend tomorrow with Preston, Claire, and Tommy. This time, however, Luis and I entered the hotel as man and wife, and we had reserved just the one room. The other time, we were only beginning to get to know one another. As we opened the door to our room, he impulsively picked me up and carried me across the doorway.

"Yikes! What are you doing?" I yelled, giggling.

"I didn't get to do that the last time," he said, laughing and tossed me down onto the bed. "We're here! It's going to be great to see the butterflies with your dad this visit. Let's enjoy!"

"And no Abbie. I guess we need that occasionally, right?"

"Absolutely. Let's make the most of it." He grinned at me mischievously. "I'll lock the door. We have an hour before the rest are due to arrive."

"Oh, you are so bad," I chided, giving him a push as he flopped on the bed beside me. "The hotel serves dinner at six. Hope the gang won't be late."

"We have plenty of time, then," he said softly, nuzzling my neck.

About forty-five minutes later, my cell phone rang. "That's probably Claire. Maybe they arrived already," I said lazily, reaching over to the bedside table to grab my phone. Luis and I had dozed off, and I didn't feel like greeting her or the guys just yet. "Hello. Mom! Hi. I wasn't expecting you to call yet. Is Abbie alright?" Instantly my gut wrenched, worrying about my baby girl so far away.

"Yes, Cassie. Abbie is just fine. I'm watching her play with her Barbie doll as we speak. I, uh, I am calling to ask you something. I, uh…"

"What is it, Mom? Just ask me. Ask me anything." I glanced over to Luis, who propped up his head in his hand, watching my face for clues.

"What is it?" Luis whispered; concern written on his face.

"Abbie is fine," I whispered, returning to Tully's call.

"Well, uh, after you and Luis left for the airport, I got to thinking how much I wanted to come with you. I really do. I don't want to miss out on seeing those butterflies, and being with all of you; Robert too, she added quickly, as if an afterthought. I heard her sigh on the phone; embarrassed to admit it. She paused, waiting for me to say something.

"Uh, okay. I wish you were here, too, Mom. But what can we do? You are there with Abbie. We are here and have scheduled the trail tour for tomorrow with Claire, Preston, and Tommy."

"Well, um, if you can hold off, I have tentatively booked a flight to Mexico City tomorrow morning. I can get to the butterfly sanctuary by early tomorrow evening. That is," she paused, clearing her throat, "if it's okay with you and Luis to have Jasmine take Abbie." She stopped again, awaiting my response.

"But how can that be? She and John teach all day until spring break starts. That's not until next week." I felt anxiety rush into my throat; I could barely talk. Abbie. My sweet baby so far away.

"Well, I thought of that. Jasmine assured me that she can drop her off with her friend until Josh and Josie get out of school and are dropped off there. The three can play together until Jasmine or John pick them all up after work. And next week is spring break, so Jasmine will be home all day." Tully tumbled out the plan, chagrined at just expressing the ideas out loud. It was so foolhardy, too last minute.

"I don't know. Luis, what do you think?" I turned to him, looking for answers. I had put the phone on speaker, so he had heard the conversation.

"Well, how many days are we talking about until spring break? Two workdays and then the weekend? Then Abbie will be with Jasmine and the kids full time, right?" Luis stared at me, attempting to be optimistic for Tully, I could tell. "This is a great opportunity for Tully, for sure," he added. By now he had gotten up, and began pacing the floor, seeming to weigh the options. "Abbie loves Josh and Josie. And Jasmine. I'm sure she will be fine," he finally concluded.

"Before I say for sure, can I talk to Jasmine?" I insisted.

"Sure. I'll have her call you right back," Tully agreed. "You won't regret this. The trip of a lifetime for all of us."

The extra few minutes between calls gave me a chance to process the whole idea. Luis too. He gave me a squeeze, and we sat on the bed discussing the new plan. I stared at the worn coverlet of the bed, absently noting the red and yellow flower swirling pattern.

In the end, Luis and I agreed, not wanting to spoil Tully's desire to join us. After all, when else would she be able to get here to see the butterflies? Then, I wondered, when did she ever express the longing to see them? What the heck? Oh well, that's Tully. Maybe at her age, she wants to go to a few places before she's too old to do so. She would be sixty-two, I calculated. Still agile and fit, able enough to ride a horse up a mountainside. How could I say no? We waited for the rest of the group to arrive before postponing the trail ride for one day, and then broke the news of the change in plans.

"No worry, girlfriend," Claire assured me. "We can just sleep in tomorrow, and then walk around the little town. Do some shopping for souvenirs. "Right, Preston?" Claire looked over at her husband, who was talking with Tommy about the village.

"What? Sure, anything you say, my sweet," Preston gave Claire a peck on her cheek.

Chapter 4

Cassie

After breakfast the next morning, all five of us, Luis and I, Claire, Preston, and Tommy, set off down the street to browse the shops. The stroll felt good since I was a bit restless, thinking about my little girl, Abbie, in Washington with Jasmine, as well as Tully, enroute somewhere between Washington and Mexico. I hung back from the group, watching all my friends, realizing how lucky I was to have them in my life. Claire and Preston took the lead, holding hands and laughing at something. They were such an unlikely couple; tall and lithe, Claire had the ivory complexion that went with her red spikey hair. Preston, on the other hand, of Asian descent, was shorter than she, stocky in build, with a shock of straight black hair. Claire could have had almost any man, but she chose sweet and dependable Preston. Cute couple. We all met on South Padre Island in Texas, where I was searching for clues to find my dad. Tommy sidled up beside Luis and me, attempting to get to know Luis a little better, I imagined.

"So, Luis," Tommy began, "do your parents and sisters still live in Puebla?"

"Sure, sure. Our family has lived there for generations."

"Oh, like my family in San Francisco. We go back about five generations before arriving in the U.S. from China." Tommy grinned, glad that he had found a commonality with Luis. Tommy was generally on the shy side, so it was significant that he was attempting conversation. Where Preston was short and stocky, Tommy was a head taller, and slight in build. The two had been friends since grade school.

"Yes? Interesting." Luis smiled back, grabbing my hand as he did so. I loved that Luis was taller than I, since I was a bit tall for a woman, and marveled that a good-looking guy like Luis fell for me years ago when I met him on top of a pyramid in Cholula, Mexico. His features, well chiseled and strong, were always ready to break out into a warm grin. I felt comfortable around him from the start.

We all stopped off in the shops together, and the morning flew by. Soon, we got hungry for lunch and grabbed tacos from a street vendor. We checked in with Jose, the trail guide who would relay to Robert that we weren't coming until tomorrow, and that Tully would be with us. I casually noticed how Jose had curly, frizzy hair like mine, but dismissed the thought. Jose took a group up every day during this season and said he would have no trouble filling our spots for the day. Slowly, we strolled back to the hotel to rest until dinner. Tully should arrive by seven, and I was restless to see her and get updates on little Abbie.

TULLY ARRIVED ON SCHEDULE AT 7:00. AS SHE STEPPED OFF THE bus, her eyes anxiously searched for me. She looked tired and wan, but her face lit up when she spotted Luis and me, waiting for her at the bus stop area. "There you are! I was afraid for a moment that perhaps I took the wrong bus to the biosphere. I'm so excited to be here!"

I swooped her up in an embrace while Luis hefted her bag and started toward the hotel. "Mom! So spontaneous that you are actually here! So how is Abbie?"

"She's great! Such a big girl, wanting to be with her cousins. She will do just fine at Jasmine's. Don't worry about her at all. Jasmine is used to children, what with her own and also a teacher. Everything will be just fine—just fine." Tully kept emphasizing the word *fine*, which made me feel a bit uneasy. "I'll have to catch you up on all the latest news, what with you being isolated up here on the mountain in Mexico."

"Oh?" *There was the worry again.* We reached the lobby of the hotel, where Claire, Preston, and Tommy waited to greet Tully. At least, I was distracted for the moment as they all greeted Tully with hugs.

"Ready for a trail ride?" Preston asked, smiling at Tully and arching his eyebrows.

"Sure, that's why I'm here. Can't wait!"

"We leave at 7:00 in the morning. So early, right? But it's a long ride and we want time to enjoy the butterflies." Preston took over the luggage as Luis and I checked Tully into the hotel for her own room. Luis said something in Spanish, indicating Tully with a glance, and the clerk nodded, bowing deferentially to Tully. He gave her a key, and we trudged up the creaky stairs to the third floor where all our rooms were located.

Chapter 5

CASSIE

I had never witnessed Tully mounted on a horse. I'm not sure she had ever actually ridden one before. She tightly grasped the reins of an older, trusty steed, while Jose gave her a cursory lesson on how to manage the animal. "Just give Apache the reins unless you need him to slow down or stop. He is a good follower and will just go with the group for the most part." Jose demonstrated with the reins, while Tully observed closely. The rest of our group was mounted and ready to shove off. Today I was assigned to a rust-colored horse named Jack. Funny how they all seemed to have American names. Perhaps it was because most of the tourists who rode up the mountain were Americans—easier I suppose. Besides our group, there were three other tourists, all from Texas, who had arrived together.

As we set out, Jose in the lead on a tall, dapple-gray, the rest of our horses knew to follow behind. Tully and her horse trailed behind Jose, and were directly in front of me, with Luis behind, while Preston, Claire, and Tommy behind Luis. The three Texans formed the rear.

The day proved to be hot, but our horses seemed used to the climate, and continued to plod one foot after the other as we ascended slowly up the mountain. Jose stopped the group at one point for a ten-minute rest but advised us not to dismount. The horses needed to know that it was just a short rest stop. I pulled out my water bottle from my pocket and took a sip. Tully turned around, smiling at me, as if to reassure me that she was okay. Soon, we resumed the climb. Around eleven o'clock, we reached the summit, and Jose directed us to dismount and tether our horses. Without words, he motioned to the trees and surrounding sky. There they were, in all their splendor: the Monarch butterflies. There were indeed hundreds, if not thousands this time, circling slowly in the air or hovering in huge clusters on trees. Their wings reflected the bright sun; orange and black beauty, more than the eye could appreciate.

The tourists were for the most part, speechless. We all grabbed our cameras or phones and began capturing the moment. Tully glanced at me, her eyes saying it all. "Spectacular," she whispered.

"I know. Unreal." The scene was so awe inspiring that all of us tourists were afraid to spoil it by speaking loudly. Silence reigned up there on the mountain top—it only seemed natural. We were the outsiders and were privileged to witness this. A few birds were the only sounds that nature provided, aside from an occasional gust of wind rustling the trees.

After about ten minutes or so, Jose spoke softly, but loud enough for all of us to hear. "We will rest our horses here and have lunch." He opened his saddlebag and pulled out the sandwiches provided for the tour. After distributing those, he tended the horses, giving them a few handfuls of oats. The horses were already nibbling on the grass and seemed content. As we ate, grouping ourselves in small circles, with the Texans forming their own circle, Jose walked to our group, and took me aside. "I told Robert you were all coming today. He's probably waiting inside the cabin when you've finished your lunch." He nodded toward the cabin which lay about five hundred feet away.

I knew that this was probably the case, but agreed that we should eat first, since the tour was on a certain schedule. "Okay, who wants to go with me?" I glanced over to Tully with a mischievous grin.

Both Tully and Luis accompanied me to the cabin. Before we reached the steps to the porch, the door swung open, and there was Robert, towering in the doorway with a grin. "Welcome to my abode," he said in his deep sonorous voice, bowing and gesturing grandly with his right arm to come in.

"Are you sure, Dad? The last time I got the door slammed in my face," I teased. It was true, but we had both gotten past that. I knew that this time, he was looking forward to our being here.

"I know, I know. That's in the past, right?" Suddenly, Robert's eyes made contact with Tully's. "Tully. Such a delight to entertain you here in my humble home. Come in, come in. I made coffee." The three of us ascended the four steps to his cabin and entered. Never in my wildest imagination did I dream I would ever get to enter my father's house. As I strode into Robert's cabin, the aroma of coffee mixed with a smokey fire in the hearth assailed my nose. It was a comforting, welcoming aroma, even though the temperature outside was not cold—probably around sixty-five degrees Fahrenheit. "Have a seat and get comfortable," Robert gestured to the living area affording a green sofa with soft cushions as well as an overstuffed floral chair. A Persian rug covered the middle of the floor, completing the cozy feel of the cabin. Tully and I sat on the sofa, while Luis plopped into the chair.

"Say, Robert, I'm just curious. How did you get this large sofa and chair up the side of the mountain?" Luis asked what we were all wondering.

As Robert brought in mugs of coffee and set them in front of us on the rough wooden coffee table he replied. "Well, I was curious as to how that happened as well. All of the furniture was here when I arrived years ago. Then I heard that there is a wagon road which cuts up through to the summit. I didn't give it too much thought, since I was focused on how the Monarchs manage to migrate to this mountain each year." Robert shrugged his shoulders and returned to the kitchen area to retrieve a plate of cookies. Interesting how he had planned our get together in his home. I glanced around, intrigued as to how my father lived. The cabin appeared to have a loft, where I assumed a bedroom was located. The open kitchen and living area were what I would expect to find in a cabin. A bookshelf lined the opposite wall of the fireplace, filled to the brim with books. I stood up and walked over to the bookshelf to read some of the titles of the books. I turned my head to read the names on their spines. Most were entomologist research volumes, thick and intimidating. A few titles appeared to be botany volumes, regarding the foliage found in mountainous regions, and some, surprisingly, looked like easy reading fiction. I guess that up here one would need a variety of reading material. "Want to check out my research books, Cassie?" Robert chuckled, catching me off guard as he set down the coffee mugs.

"Oh! No, I, uh, was just browsing. Thanks anyway, Dad." *My face felt hot; why did that bother me that he asked me that?* I knew he was a private person; perhaps I felt like I was violating his space somehow.

"So, Tully, how did you manage to spring free and make it all the way up here?" Robert directed his gaze at Tully, smiling as he took a sip of his coffee.

"Well, I just asked Jasmine if she and John could take over caring for Abbie, and then booked a flight, all in the same day."

Tully tittered, as if hearing the impulsiveness of her decision as it was uttered out loud.

"Good. Glad you did. No use letting an opportunity slip by, especially at our age, right?" Again, the intensity of his eyes toward her, taking another sip off his cup to cover his smile.

"Uh, yes. That's what I decided," Tully admitted, a bit nervous, as she too, swallowed a little of her coffee. She set her cup down on the coffee table, as if punctuating the thought. "So, Cassie, what do you think of Abbie going to the zoo with Jasmine and John? Good idea?" The change of subject was abrupt—obvious.

"Yeah, sure, Mom. She will love that." I gave her a questioning look. *What the heck? Of course it is a good idea.*

"I'll bet Abbie is growing like a weed by now," Robert interjected, veering away from the awkward moment.

"Yes." Tully looked down as she said this, afraid it seemed, to meet Robert's gaze.

We chatted for a few more minutes, but all too soon our time ran out, and Luis mentioned that we better rejoin the tour group. He had looked out the window, and saw the others standing up, ambling toward their assigned horses. It was difficult to tear ourselves away from Robert; after the arduous journey up the mountain, we hated to say goodbye. I could tell that Robert felt the same. He looked dejected—almost sad to see us leave. "Say," he said suddenly, "I need to go into town this week to check out some supplies I need for gardening. How long will you all be in town?"

"Well, uh, we could stay on a few days if the hotel isn't booked," I offered, glancing over to Luis and Tully, who both nodded in agreement.

"Okay then. I'll be down in two days if Jose can bring an extra horse for me. How does that sound?" Robert jumped up, clearing our mugs of coffee, as if excited at the prospect.

"Yes, that will be nice. We can extend our visit with you," Luis agreed.

"Can you stay in town a couple of days at our hotel?" I looked at him wistfully, wishing it could be.

"Why don't you check that possibility when you make sure of your rooms—reserve one for me."

Tully smiled shyly, nodding to Robert as if to say she was hoping for that too.

"Well, we have to get going. They are getting on the horses now," Luis reminded us, looking anxiously out the window. He shook hands with Robert, and I got up from the sofa to give Dad a hug. Then he moved closer to Tully and gave her an awkward side hug. We quickly said our goodbyes and lumbered down the steps of the cabin and strode rapidly towards our horses.

Preston, Claire, and Tommy were assembled with the tour group, already mounted on their horses, awaiting our arrival to rejoin the riders. As our horses ambled down the mountain trail that day in March of 2020, little did we realize how rapidly the world below us had already begun to change forever.

Chapter 6

Cassie

"So, did you hear about the pandemic?" I looked over my iced tea to Robert, who had just met up with us in the hotel eating area.

"What's that? I haven't heard anything. Remember, I just came down from the mountain cabin about an hour ago." Robert arrived two days after we had descended from the summit to the village. By then, I had already heard from Jasmine, who filled us in on the Coronavirus pandemic, which was rapidly gaining a stranglehold on the entire world. As far as we could tell, here in the isolated mountainous region of the Biosphere, nothing had changed yet; no one seemed to know much about the pandemic or had contracted the virus.

"Well, according to Jasmine, entire cities are going into lockdown. People can't enter stores except for those offering essential services, such as groceries or medicine; restaurants are closed, and schools have locked their doors. The few stores open for essential services have wait lines, due to limits on the numbers of people allowed in at one time. Hospitals don't allow visitors; church services are cancelled as well as weddings and funerals. Sports events are viewed online only, and other crowded events, such as concerts, are cancelled. Students are required to study online at home, and office employees are working dressed in their pajamas from laptops on their kitchen tables. Kids are home, workers are home—it's getting weird and crazy out there." Luis finished, and then took a bite out of his burrito, touching his lips with a napkin.

"What in the world?" Robert looked at us, aghast in surprise.

"Yeah, guess it's true. We need to get on the internet to see exactly what is going on."

"Well, if your phone isn't connecting, I know that the pharmacy down the street has a computer we can use. It usually works." Robert sounded helpful, but at the same time, it was humorous—so backwards for the year 2020 to have to use a business computer to get online.

"Usually works?" Oh my. Where are we?" It was strange to be so out of touch with civilization.

"You know—this is a third world country on top of a remote mountain. What do you suppose?" Robert chuckled good naturedly, snatching up the bill for our lunch before Luis had a chance.

"Let me at least get the tip," Luis insisted, plopping down some cash.

As we suspected, when we attempted to use our phones for the internet, there were no bars for connection. So, we made our way down the street to the pharmacy. There was already a waiting line for the use of the computer—and the store charged usage by the minute. We got in line. It was a bit unorganized, with no wait list, so we just took turns standing in the queue. An hour or so later, we were able to read news from the U.S., and Washington, Oregon, and California in particular. Sure enough, those states were all in lock down, as well as some other states.

"What will we do now?" Luis voiced the question we were all asking ourselves. Tully, Preston, Claire, and Tommy had joined us in the pharmacy as well. We all felt so out of touch up on the remote mountain top. We were gripped by the fear of uncertainty; the virus was sweeping across the globe, killing thousands of those in its path. *Indeed, what will we do?* I wondered. I worried about Abbie, and desperately thought of the worst. I wanted to rush home to her to protect her. *What if she contracted the virus? Or Jasmine, John, or their kids, Josh and Josie? Would they be hospitalized, or worse?*

"How will we return home? Will customs allow us into the U.S. from Mexico when our plane gets in? Or are we even allowed to leave from Mexico?" Luis continued to ask the questions I was afraid to ask. "What if one of us gets sick before our plane is due to depart from Mexico? Then what?"

Before the terrifying news, our plans had been to leave Angangueo in two days and head to Puebla to visit Luis' family for a few days and go sightseeing. Luis and I were to stay at his parents' home and the rest, including Tully and Robert, would go to a hotel. Actually, I had hoped to stay in a hotel, but his mother, Maria, insisted we stay with them. Now, I wondered if the virus would follow us to Puebla. Were people contracting it there as well? Were we risking our health and Luis' family to stay with them? Soon, we would have more answers. We just needed to get back to civilization.

"Okay, let's go back to the hotel and regroup. Meet in the restaurant there for drinks?" Luis was a calming force for all of us. We agreed and ambled slowly back to the hotel. There really was nothing we could do right away since our return flight had been scheduled ahead of time. No doubt it would be pandemonium at airports right now, and difficult, if not impossible, to get a flight home ahead of our itinerary.

Chapter 7

Cassie

"Do you suppose they will recognize us?" Luis and I had arrived at his parents' house two days later, standing on the doorstep, donned with face masks purchased in a pharmacy in Puebla. I looked at Luis and giggled.

"No worries there," Luis laughed, his voice slightly muffled from behind the mask, when just at that moment the door swung open and he was embraced in his mother's hug, his cheeks covered in her kisses.

"Come in, come in," Maria urged, grabbing hold of me for a hug and kiss as well. I stood stiffly in the doorway, enduring her affection. I still had trouble getting accustomed to his family's demonstrative show of love. Maria had no mask on, but we kept on ours, entering the house. Soon, we were surrounded by Viviana and Mercedes, also showering Luis and me with hugs and kisses. The aroma of dinner wafted towards us, fragrant with beef and spices. "I see you have heard about the pandemic. It's here in the city already; actually, many have been hospitalized. Some have died. Do as you wish with the mask wearing. We will wear one when out but decided to be normal in our own home." Maria smiled, understanding written on her face. "But you two decide for yourselves."

Luis searched for my reaction, hidden behind my mask, but my eyes were enough. "Thank you, Mom. We will talk about it later. For now, we'll leave them on until we eat."

"Yes, thank you, Maria. I'm so worried about coming down with it before we can fly home. It's really scary, thinking of Abbie in another country with this going on. I feel so—uh, helpless."

"I understand. You are the mother. You need to be home during this outbreak and do all you can to protect your little one. I know the feeling—I'm a mother, too." Maria gazed at me sympathetically and grasped my hand in hers. Tears came to my eyes. I couldn't help it. The anxiety welled up no matter how hard I tried for it not to. "There, there. It's going to be alright. You'll see." Maria patted my hand and then returned to her cooking in the kitchen.

There were no words for how I felt just then. I had this overwhelming rush of home sickness. I needed to hold Abbie in my arms. I wanted to touch the softness of her curly, frizzy hair; kiss her pudgy, little cheeks. I longed to rock her, sing to her, read to her. She seemed like a distant memory already. She was so far away—impossible to get to at the moment. There were so many uncertainties of how to return to her. I reached into my bag and found a tissue, loudly blowing my nose.

Luis looked over at me, startled by the noise, concern in his eyes. "Perhaps we could call Abbie after dinner," he suggested. "It may help you just to hear Abbie and be reassured that she is doing okay. Or we could even try to face time her. Then you could see her as well." He brightened at the idea, and I took another tissue, honking my nose a few more times.

"Sounds good," I slowly admitted. "Let's try that."

"Yes! A wonderful idea," Maria said, stirring something in a large pot. Mercedes agreed, nodding vigorously.

At that moment, Viviana took my hand, leading me to the upholstered chair in the living room. "Here, Cassie, sit and let us get dinner on the table. You will feel better after you eat something." She smiled encouragingly, gently pushing me into the soft cushions of the chair. I allowed myself to relax and put my feet up onto the ottoman. I put my head back onto the headrest, listening to their voices in the background, as the three women prepared our meal. The warmth of the room, the sounds and smells of cooking soothed my mind, and I drifted off for a few minutes.

I awoke with a start when Luis spoke softly, saying, "Cassie, honey, let's come to the table and eat." He took my hand to help me out of the chair.

"Oh! I must've fallen asleep." My legs felt like rubber, as I made my way to the dining room. I realized then that I hadn't slept much since we heard the devastating news of lockdowns where Abbie and my family were located.

After dinner, we tried to call Jasmine to put Abbie on the phone and arrange a face time call. Oddly, there was no answer. We attempted several times, but it always went to voice mail. I had to give up trying to call and prepared for bed. Mercedes gave us her room and she walked down the hall to bunk with Viviana. It took me over an hour to finally drift off, only to be awakened with a recurring nightmare of the pandemic. I had read online and heard on the TV since arriving in Puebla of the horrors of people dying all over the world, with not enough ventilators in hospitals. In my nightmare, I was struggling to breathe through a ventilator mask. Moaning and thrashing around, I finally woke up. At first, I was disoriented and in the dark, forgetting where I was. Then it hit me: I was an alien, visiting in Mexico. Did they have enough ventilators here if one of us got sick and needed one? What if Luis or I came down with Covid while enroute home? Or could we even leave if we wanted to? I continued to toss and turn, sleepless for much of the remaining hours of night. Every time I closed my eyes, I saw my little Abbie with arms outstretched, pleading "Mommy, Mommy." She was crying—inconsolable.

Chapter 8

CASSIE

"It's beautiful up here!" Claire exclaimed as we all reached the summit of the pyramid of Cholula. We were a large group this morning, since Tommy and Preston had come along, as well as Mercedes and Viviana, Tully, and Robert. The first time I ascended these same steps, I was a lone tourist and journalist. I had met Luis on this very summit, years ago. The memory flashed back, and I reached out to grab Luis' hand. He grinned back at me, also remembering the moment we had met.

We were all out of breath, having just mounted hundreds of steps, but were rewarded with a view of the vista in the distance of the looming peaks of Popocatepetl and Iztaccihuatl. The latter, in English, was referred to as "White Woman," or "Sleeping Woman." The mountain supposedly resembled a woman lying on her back, often covered in snow. As we gazed into the distance, we each observed that it did indeed slightly resemble a sleeping woman.

"The first mountain in the distance, the one called "Popo" for Popocatepetl, is still an active volcano." Luis was our official tour guide of the day. "Also, there is a legend regarding both mountains." Claire was the one holding a map of the pyramid and examined it closely. She pointed out different places, and we all bent our heads over the map while Luis explained the various areas. The map was in Spanish, so he was very helpful in interpreting it for us. Only a portion of the pyramid had been excavated thus far, but archeologists painstakingly kept up the work, and bit by bit, new sections were exposed. Slowly, we walked around the perimeter of the pyramid at the summit, taking in the landscape from all directions. It was a clear day as usual there, and our sight stretched as far as the horizon. Luis filled in details about the area, when at last, we descended the long stairs, the stairs zigzagging down in several switchbacks. The steps wound their way around the pyramid, and we concluded our tour after another thirty minutes.

"Is there a good place to eat?" Preston asked.

Luis glanced at his watch. "Right. It's past lunch time. Sure, there are many good places, and most are inexpensive in this village."

"Okay, let's find one," Preston said, grinning and grabbing Claire's hand. "I'm starving!"

"You always are," Claire chided good naturedly.

Chapter 9

CASSIE

"Sometimes we should express our gratitude for the small and simple things like the scent of rain, the taste of your favorite food, or the sound of a loved one's voice."

—Joseph B. Wirthlin

The tour of the Cholula Pyramid distracted my mind for a while. I didn't worry about Abbie during the four hours or so that we spent there. The moment we returned to Luis' family home, however, the images in my mind returned with a vengeance. I pictured Abbie once more, sick with Covid, crying out for me, arms outstretched. No one could console her because I wasn't there. I had drifted into a fitful nap, awakening moaning, drenched in sweat. "I want to go home. Home," I moaned.

"Wake up, Cass." Luis was shaking my shoulder. "You're dreaming again."

"Wha—what?" I opened my eyes reluctantly, not wanting the nightmare to stop. It had to go on until I could manage to arrive home with Abbie. "Where is she? When will we get there?"

"Sh-sh-sh. It's okay. You were dreaming again. Dinner is nearly ready, and Mom has fixed us a delicious meal of enchiladas. Why don't you get up and splash some water on your face? You'll feel better." Luis took hold of my elbow and brought me to a sitting position on the bed.

"I'm so tired. I still didn't sleep much last night. I worry about Abbie when I'm awake and when I'm trying to sleep." I staggered into the bathroom to splash water on my face and looked at myself in the mirror. Dark circles surrounded my eyes, and my hair was an even bigger frizzy mess than usual. I attempted to tame my hair with water on my fingers, massaging the moisture into the ends of my mane. It helped a little, but there was no hope for the dark circles. I changed out of my sweaty tee shirt into a fresh blue blouse and headed downstairs to the dining room. I put a smile on my face, hoping it would pass as appearing pleasant, and tackled yet another meal with Luis' family. I just wanted to go somewhere to hide and be alone, but it was impossible here with his outgoing and loving family.

"So, Cassie, tell us about what you do with the newspaper company," Maria prompted. Inwardly I groaned but attempted a bright face, swallowing hard. As I described my role at the newspaper as a journalist, mostly of feature stories about interesting people in the community of Lincoln City, Oregon, Maria and the girls listened with rapt attention. Esteban looked on politely, nodding ever so often as he chewed his enchiladas.

"Cassie is being too modest," Luis interjected. "She writes splendidly. I love reading her articles. The paper comes out two times a week, and she manages to write something for every issue, plus look after Abbie and me." Luis turned to smile at me as I weakly acknowledged his comment with a nod. All I really wanted to talk about was my worry about Abbie and being here during a pandemic. I just wanted to run out of the room, pack my bag, and take a taxi to the airport. But the airport was over two hours away.

I pushed the food around on my plate with a fork, my appetite gone. Anxiety clenched at my stomach, and I couldn't possibly eat another bite. "Cassie dear, is the food to your liking?" Maria noticed, of course.

"Yes, yes, it's delicious. Thank you. I—I don't seem to have an appetite this evening." I still saw Abbie in tears at the edge of my mind. I couldn't shake the image.

"Sure, sure. Just eat what you feel like. I understand. Being away from home and your child isn't always easy."

"We'll try to call Abbie again this evening. Maybe we will get through this time." Luis sounded overly chirpy, but he was trying to reassure me. The meal continued, mainly in silence, with only the sound of scraping plates with forks. I was so relieved when I could excuse myself and go to the room Luis and I were sharing. I threw myself down on the bed, the tears flowing like a gushing waterfall.

Luis joined me after a few minutes and sat down on the edge of the bed beside me. "Honey, I know it's difficult for you to be in Mexico with the Covid outbreak, but this is where we are. At least we are here now with my family. It could be worse. Shall we try to call Abbie again now?" He took my hand, beseeching my face. I could read concern behind his eyes.

"Okay. Try," I sniffed, reaching for a tissue.

This time, the call didn't even go through. It was like the whole system was overloaded with too many people trying to reach loved ones. I sank into the pillow, my tears renewed. "I'm going to see what our chances are for booking a flight back earlier than we have scheduled. I'll let you know what I find out." Luis tiptoed from the room and softly closed the door behind him. I lay there staring at the ceiling, wondering where all of this would lead. I desperately wanted to return home to my little girl.

Chapter 10

CASSIE

"I love the smell of rain, and I love the sound of the ocean waves."

—Amy Purdy

I scarcely slept all night. Luis wasn't even able to get through to the airline, either by phone or online. Those systems were down too, it seemed. To reach the airport in person was more than two hours away by bus. That didn't seem possible right now, either. We were stuck, at least for the time being. I felt cut off from my world—from my baby girl, my sister, and home. Home. I truly longed for home. It even smelled different here in Puebla. The air was tainted with dry dust, hot spices, and soured food. Home in the U.S. Northwest smelled fresh from the rains that invariably arrived, causing the earth to release its fragrance, blending with the clean and vibrant scent of fir trees. Here in Puebla, there were very few trees or vegetation—lots of asphalt and spicey cooking odors wafted from windows or street vendors. Then there was the noise: street traffic, the vendors hawking their wares from deafening megaphones, roosters crowing from nearly every dusty dry yard, dogs barking incessantly. Lawns bore the rock-hard clay surface from lack of rain. I longed to hear the tall fir trees swaying gently in the breeze, rains pelting the rooftops with their cleansing waters, the excess dropping to the soil, which was softened by their moisture.

Most of all, I yearned to hear my Abbie's peals of laughter as she reached out to catch the rain drops or pet our cat's soft fur. As I smiled in my sleep, watching Abbie, I felt something on my left side. "Cassie, time to get up, Sweetheart." I had drifted off, my reverie interrupted by Luis, shaking my shoulder to awaken me. His face hovered over me, grinning as usual.

"Wh—what? Let me sleep. I want to see Abbie in my dreams some more." I rolled away from him, suddenly realizing something. I was definitely homesick—and I resented his intrusion. I was irritated by his constant chirpiness. Of course, he was happy—he was staying here in his childhood home, surrounded by all his family! Even amid this horrid new pandemic, he was home with his loved ones. Me? What did I have? Nothing but disgusting foreign sounds and smells and the possibility of contracting a deadly disease in a distant land. Under it all, I knew I had a new fear—contracting the dread virus and becoming a patient in a hospital in Mexico. "Go away! Let me alone!" Escape in sleep was all I had.

"Okay, but the rest of us—Tully, Robert, Claire, Preston, Tommy, and my sisters—are going to meet up downtown. We'll tour the cathedral and then get lunch. Want to come?" Luis stared at me with his pleading, dark eyes. He looked so winsome. How could I say no?

"Oh, alright. I'll get up. But I need to shower first. It will take me awhile to put myself together."

"Sure, sure. No problem. Mom has coffee and breakfast waiting, too."

"Well, I don't want much. Just coffee and toast." I knew by now that "toast" here meant the hard, toasted kind like melba toast. But it was okay. I was getting used to it.

The outing downtown turned out to be a nice diversion from my constant obsession over Abbie. Seeing our friends turned out to be good therapy. It helped to see Tully, or Mom, as well. I expressed my worry to her as we strolled the market together. It was entertaining to watch her buying a few things such as handcrafted jewelry and pottery. I just wasn't in the mood to make purchasing decisions myself. Tully saw the concern written on my countenance, taking my hand and squeezing it. "Don't worry about Abbie, Sweetie. It will all work out. Jasmine is so good with children, you know. She has her own, plus is a teacher of children." Tully grinned at me reassuringly, trying to cheer me.

"I know, Mom. But you can imagine how difficult it is to be a mom and be so far away. Very scary."

"Sure, sure. But Abbie is with your sister, like I said, and your husband and I are here with you. It's going to be okay…really."

"Mom, I have nightmares about this every night. The uncertainty of the pandemic is so different. The world seems to be changing its rules—too fast."

"Yes, but there's not a whole lot we can do about that. Just pray that Abbie is okay and try to make the best of things while we are here."

"You're right. I just don't know how to be at peace with it all." Tully took my hand, squeezed it, but said no more. What more was there to say? Right then, Robert caught up with us. He had been browsing with a vendor offering hand tooled leather items, such as belts and purses. It appeared that he had purchased a belt. He grabbed Tully's hand and began swinging her around.

"Stop!" Tully giggled like a schoolgirl. I saw her look of rapture as she stared into Robert's eyes.

"Look what I got!" Robert said, holding up a finely crafted belt. "It's beautiful, don't you think?" He attempted to try it on, all the while, Tully laughed and took hold of it, pulling him even closer to her. I didn't know what to think. They were acting like teenagers. Kind of disgusting, at least to me. Luis and I never got like that.

As we all leisurely strolled around the market area, I observed Tommy walking close to Viviana the entire time. Interesting development. I continued to observe them, their heads bent close, talking softly to one another, laughing, and making a few purchases together.

Well, well, well. Everyone was pairing up. Naturally, Claire was accompanied by her husband, Preston, as they also seemed to be having a good time. I grasped Luis by the hand, deciding it was time for me too, to try to savor the moment. I had been a pain in Luis' side, no doubt. I owed him a carefree afternoon. Who knows? Maybe I could escape my inner turmoil by letting go while touring around like everyone else.

"Say, Cassie, look at this!" Claire exclaimed, as she and Preston held up a hand painted plate, crafted and painted in the style renown here in Puebla. "We got it at a bargain! Preston knows how to dicker with merchants."

"It's lovely. Can he buy me one?" The pattern was done in blues and oranges. I loved it.

"Sure. I'll see what I can do," Preston retorted. Soon, I too was the proud owner of a hand-painted plate in Puebla's colors. The merchant carefully wrapped it in newsprint, bagged it, and we sauntered on down the marketplace. Before I knew it, I was laughing, reveling in our friends, the sunny afternoon, and all the wares offered for sale. The street vendors offered jewelry in gold and silver, pottery, traditional Mexican clothing, scarves, blankets, wooden carvings, candles—you name it.

We left the market area and entered the towering cathedral. The door was open, a marvel to me, as an American. In the U.S., most churches opened their doors only for services. Here in Mexico, the chapels and cathedrals functioned as open refuges to anyone who wished to enter the peaceful solitude. As we all softly tiptoed inside, the cavernous interior echoed our footsteps. Silently we made our way down the aisle towards the front. I was awestruck, as always, by the vast magnitude of the tall ceilinged structure. Statues of saints and angels glared down at us solemnly, as if in disapproval of the echoing footsteps we made as a group, shuffling to the furthest point up front before mutely sitting down on the hard, wooden benches. I remembered the first time I visited here in Puebla and Luis brought me to this holy sanctuary. I smiled to myself as I observed Claire, Preston, and Tommy riveting their eyes and craning their necks to take it all in. Tully simply bowed her head, as did Robert. I recalled at that moment how Tully had converted to the Catholic church. That was the reason I was baptized Catholic as an infant. I didn't know much about my real father, Robert, and wondered if he too, had been inside a cathedral before. He appeared to be accustomed to the atmosphere here. I glanced beside me and saw that Luis was already on the kneeler with his head bowed, hands in supplication, in silent prayer. I decided to do that as well. After all, I was stressed and worried about Abbie. Praying here in this holy sanctuary seemed a good idea. I knelt down, took a deep breath, and bowed my head as well, becoming introspective. *"Dear God, please protect my Abbie. She's so far away, and I'm helpless to be with her. Please help us to return home as soon as possible. Amen."*

When I raised my head, I felt that a burden had been lifted—at least, for the moment. I glanced around at the rest of our group, and it appeared that everyone else was waiting for Luis and me to get up from the kneeler to leave. Quietly, we all paraded back out into the sweltry sunshine, our souls a bit refreshed.

The day sped by, and soon, we returned by bus to our respective housing. The others got out at their hotel, but Luis and I and his sisters, Viviana and Mercedes, traveled on to his parents' house for dinner and a place to sleep. I would have preferred to get a meal at the hotel with Tully and our friends, but Luis' parents were expecting us.

Chapter 11

CASSIE

"Rain is grace; rain is the sky descending to the earth; without rain, there would be no life."

—John Updike

What the heck was going on at the hotel when Luis and I weren't around? It seemed that there was a rapidly spiraling romance occurring with Tully and Robert. What's more, Tommy and Viviana were strolling around holding hands, although Viviana, of course, returned home at night to her parents' where Luis and I stayed. Sometimes, she arrived late, with Tommy saying goodbye to her on the doorstep. I smirked to myself, as we watched it all happening whenever we all got together. Funny, Luis and I had fallen in love here as well, years prior. Claire and Preston had also developed their attraction for one another in Mexico when we went to the Monarch Sanctuary years before. There was definitely something in the air here, I concluded. In a good way, I suppose. The whole idea of our friends and family discovering romance helped keep my anxiety at bay, at least, for the time being.

Each morning, after Luis and I ate breakfast, he attempted to call Jasmine and Abbie. So far, we haven't been able to get through.

Phone lines were still overloaded. It was during midday, as we had journeyed out to the market to pick up some food items for Maria, that my phone rang. "Jasmine, is that you?" The reception was sketchy.

"Yes, it's me. Abbie is okay. John and I are okay. Josh and Josie are okay, too. Uh, it's about Grandpa Ray."

My breath caught in my throat. I had heard of how easily the virus took down the elderly. "Yes, is he alright?" I had visions of him gasping for air beneath a ventilator.

"Well, no." Jasmine's voice broke. "He's…he's in the I.C.U. at the hospital. Corona virus." I heard Jasmine crying, her voice choked.

"Have you seen him? Is he going to be alright?" I had forgotten all about my aging grandparents and their vulnerability in my overarching concern for Abbie. Guilt washed over me, a flood of emotions, and so removed from home.

"No—no we haven't seen him. No one is allowed in the hospital except for patients and hospital staff. And the hospitals are overrun with sick people, most with Covid symptoms. Some are in beds, lying in hallways. The patient rooms are full." At that, Jasmine broke off, overcome with sadness.

"Oh, so horrible! I wish I were there. I hate being stuck here in Mexico during this pandemic."

"There's nothing you could do here, anyway. I just thought I would attempt to call and was able to get through. I'll keep you posted."

"So—so how is Grandma?" I asked desperately.

"She's strong. She will be okay, I hope. Gotta go. I'm in my classroom with students at the moment but was able to get through just now somehow. Bye." With that, the line went dead.

So that was it. "Grandpa is in I.C.U. with Covid," I said flatly. The tears fell, but there was nothing I could do. I was a world away.

Grandpa Ray passed away in three more days, although we didn't receive any news from Jasmine until a week later. We still couldn't place calls through from Mexico, but she was finally able to call us from the U.S. There was no funeral. Funerals were not allowed, she said, due to the lockdown. When I heard the heartbreaking news, I stayed in my room the entire rest of the day. This continued for the next three days, as I became inconsolable, refusing to eat anything more than toast and coffee. I just had no energy to face Luis' family and put on a fake smile. If only I could return home. I could hold Abbie, visit Jasmine and Grandma, go through the grief together.

When we told Tully about her father, she too, became lethargic. She didn't want to tour anymore or go anywhere. She hovered in her hotel room alone, only going out to eat in the hotel's dining area. I never saw her look so sad before. It was unbearable to see her this way. It seemed worse than my own sorrow.

This latest news made getting back home more urgent somehow. All of us as a family needed one another. Luis got up early on the fourth morning after hearing that my grandfather had passed, determined to catch a bus to the Mexico City airport. "Cassie, Love, I'm going to travel to the airport and see what I can do to get us earlier tickets back to the states, even though by now, our present return tickets are for ten days from now."

"You are?" I sat up, rubbing my eyes, not sure what I was hearing. I hadn't really slept much; just tossed and turned, picturing my poor grandpa suffering alone in a hospital. Dying alone. The images were still there in my mind. I tried to jerk myself awake. "Wh-when?"

"I'm leaving now. I'll take a cab to the bus station and from there, take a bus to the airport. The bus to Mexico City takes about two hours, so I should be back home before bedtime." He sounded so confident; I couldn't protest.

"Oh, okay. But be careful and wear a mask at all times."

"I will. I'll let Mom know that I'm leaving so she won't fix breakfast for me. Don't worry. I'll be back before you know it." With that, he pecked me on the cheek and shut the door with a firm click. I sat there in bed, thinking about our journey here thus far. It was certainly turning out differently than we had planned. But then, who planned for a pandemic outbreak?

I dressed quickly and entered the kitchen area, determined to greet Luis' family, and eat with them at long last. After all, I thought brightly, perhaps we would be able to return home soon. I would need my strength to travel. I put on a smile and took the steps downstairs with a lightness in my feet.

Chapter 12

TULLY

"Tears of joy are like the summer rain drops pierced by sunbeams."

—*Hosea Ballou*

How could this have happened? We left the States for a fun tour of the biosphere of the Monarchs, and a horrible pandemic began while we were away. Now my father is dead, and I wasn't even by his side to tell him goodbye or to say that I love him. My mother needs me—Jasmine needs me. I feel so very helpless. I must get back to help them with final arrangements, even though there won't be a funeral.

I remained in my hotel room, deciding to order room service of coffee and a pastry. I ate nothing more for the rest of the day. I lay in my bed, alternating between weeping and reminiscing of my growing up years with my beloved father. The memories haunted me, at one point, conjuring up the day of my marriage to Sean. I was nervous and had misgivings on my wedding day. Only my father, Ray, had been there for me, offering support and love. My mother, Vicki, remained emotionally distant, upset with me up until moments before walking down the aisle, presumably because of my premature decision to wed Sean. We were too young, Vicki claimed. I was barely nineteen at the time.

I was crying, hoping that I could dash out of the church before I had to say I do. I stood in the foray, paralyzed to the spot. I just couldn't do it. Then Dad walked over, smiled at me, lifted my veil, and kissed me full on the lips. I don't remember him even kissing me on the cheek before. I was moved by his demonstration of fatherly love, and his strength gave me the courage I needed. Without speaking, he took my arm, and we started down the aisle, all eyes on us. I made it to the altar with Dad's support.

Dad was the one who gave me the confidence to drive a stick shift. I remember him calmly putting his hand over mine as I gripped the gear shift knob. Gently, he helped me to put the car in first gear, and then, as I slowly accelerated, he guided me into second. I gazed up for a second at Dad, who was smiling his encouragement.

"You can do this," he proclaimed. And I did.

Finally, I remembered the time that he was the one who was there for me when I was taken to emergency before surgery. I had been in a car accident. I should have been terrified, but he was there, speaking softly into my ear, reassuring me. He was always there when I needed him most.

Now, Dad had been abandoned in his hour of need. No one in the family had been permitted to go to his hospital room as he lay dying. Worst of all, I wasn't even in the U.S. He had died alone.

I wept until no more tears would come. Guilt racked my brain, making me feel so helpless. Exhausted, I fell into a fitful sleep, imagining my beloved father struggling to breathe, a ventilator attached to his face.

Chapter 13

CASSIE

The lockdown in Puebla and most of Mexico began the next day. When we arose, we saw the news of the lockdown on television. "What does it really mean?" Maria asked. How can this be true? So, all businesses are on lockdown except those offering food or basic services? But what about churches? And schools? What about that?" Appalled, Maria looked from Luis to me, demanding answers.

"Not sure, Mom. All I know is from the internet that the same thing already exists in most of the U.S."

"So, for how long? What do we do in the meantime?" Maria asked in desperation.

"We isolate, and we wait."

Hotels were affected as well. No more food was available in the hotel dining room, or any restaurant, for that matter. Tully, Robert, Preston, Claire, and Tommy were forced to purchase food from vendors and eat in their rooms. Everywhere—on the street, in the hotel, a hush pervaded. Few people ventured out, and those who did possessed a fearful look in their eyes above their masks.

THE KNOCKING ON TULLY'S HOTEL ROOM DOOR CONTINUED. "Who's there?" Tully called out, throwing on her bathrobe.

"Robert. May I come in?"

"Just a moment." Tully fumbled with the belt on her robe and paused in the mirror to see how her hair looked. *Disheveled, for sure. And dark circles under my eyes.* Slowly, she ambled to the door, and undid the chain lock and deadbolt. "I'm not presentable, but come in."

Robert stepped inside, closed the door, and grabbed Tully in an embrace. "You look beautiful to me." Quickly he planted a kiss on her lips. "How are you doing now? I know your dad's passing has been difficult, especially your having to be here in Mexico. I'm so sorry."

"Yes, it has been. But sit down," she offered, gesturing to one of the two chairs which were stationed by a small table. "Uh, sorry. All I have to offer is water."

"Perfect. Thank you." He took the proffered bottle of water and sipped on it while watching Tully's face.

Silently, they sat across the table from one another. Awkward moments passed. "I'm not a good host this morning, I'm afraid. I have no words for how I'm feeling." Tully paused, feeling the tears just under the surface.

"That's understandable. Don't worry. I just wanted to see you—to make sure you are okay. And—hoping you will a me accompany me on a walk. I think there is no lockdown for that," he chuckled, trying to make light of the new restrictions.

Tully grinned a little over her water bottle and took a swallow to give her time to respond. "Well, I suppose I could muster up the energy to do that much. I need about thirty minutes to get ready. As you can see, I'm not dressed for the day." She pointed to her white robe, feeling embarrassed at her messy appearance, her hair askew, no makeup yet.

"Certainly. I'll just hang out in the lobby and wait for you. Thanks for the water," he said smiling, more in jest than serious. He gave her a little side hug and turned to leave.

Chapter 14

LUIS

I returned to my parents' home around midnight. With heavy steps, I plodded up the walk to the door and knocked. I heard a slow shuffling, and then my father, Esteban, unlocked the deadbolt and let me in. "Good news, I hope?" Dad yawned, having been awakened by the doorbell. He tousled his hair, which was standing on end from sleeping.

I hesitated, not sure where to begin. "Well, no, Dad. Not good news. Not only did I not get earlier tickets, but the airline agent also said that in most probability, our current return tickets will not be honored. They aren't allowing people to leave the country yet. It's a pandemic. So, who knows when we will be allowed to return to the States?" I collapsed in a chair at the kitchen table; exhaustion written on my face; I was certain.

"Here, let's have something to drink and think about this," Dad offered. "What do you want? Hot tea or something stronger?"

"Just some tea; thanks, Dad."

"Suit yourself. Think I'll go for something stronger."

THE MORNING SUN AWAKENED ME FROM A FITFUL NIGHT. I WAS

so frustrated with the news I had to impart to Cassie. She had been asleep when I came in last night, so I decided to reveal the bad news during the light of day. I looked down at Cassie, still sleeping. She appeared so peaceful in slumber. Too bad I had to disturb her tranquility. I tiptoed out of the bedroom, closing the door soundlessly.

"Luis, is that you?" Cassie stirred, hearing my retreating footsteps.

"Uh, yes, Sweetie. Just rest a bit more. We'll talk over coffee, okay?" I felt nervous, dreading the conversation and tears to come.

Cassie yawned, and replied sluggishly, "Sure. Later." Then she turned over and fell asleep again. I breathed a sigh of relief, heading down the stairs to the kitchen to grab some coffee. Maria was there, frying an egg. The pungent aroma of coffee permeated the air.

"Good morning, my son. Are you hungry? How did it go yesterday at the airport?" She continued to flip the egg, put down the spatula, and poured me a cup of coffee. "Here you go."

"Uh, I'll tell you in a while. I just need this coffee first," I replied, anxious for a distraction before imparting the news. "I need some fresh air. I think I'll step outside a moment and sip on this." I carried my cup outside in one hand, my cell phone in the other. Doing a Google search, I found the phone number of the U.S. Consulate in Puebla and dialed the number. I had to select several options and was placed on hold for about five minutes. Finally, a person came on the line, and I explained our situation. Soon, I grinned and nodded my head, and asked the woman on the other end to hold a moment while I grabbed a pen and paper from inside the house. "Um hm, I see," I replied, scribbling madly on the scrap of paper. By now, I was back in the kitchen, and Maria was watching me anxiously. "Gracious. Er, thank you." I disconnected the phone and attempted to act as if nothing much of consequence was learned.

"So, what did you find out, Luis?" Maria's eyes bored into mine, demanding an answer.

"Oh, just some good news for Cassie. Probably not so good for you." I grinned mischievously, sitting down at the kitchen table with a plate of eggs and tortillas. The sausages were already on a platter in the center of the table. At that moment, Cassie appeared, sleepy-eyed, but curiosity getting the best of her sleep time.

"What good news?" Cassie asked, rubbing her eyes, and sitting down with coffee in hand. Her hair stood on end; the Afro was extra frizzy in the mornings before she had a chance to work with it.

"Well, first I have to say that the airline was a bit misinformed. Yesterday they told me that no one can leave the country at the present time. However," Luis rushed on to explain as Cassie started to look dejected, "just now I called the U.S. Consulate here in Puebla and they said that citizens from other countries may return to their respective countries if visiting here in Mexico." I glanced from Maria to Cassie, observing mixed reactions.

"Oh! How wonderful! So, we can go home, right?" Cassie looked at me brightly, clutching my hand.

"Yes, according to them, at least. Unless" I added, "a person tests positive for Covid twenty-four hours prior to departure."

Maria just sat there, taking it all in, disappointment yet understanding written on her face. "Of course, you want to get back as soon as possible to see your little one. I understand." She smiled graciously.

"So, how do we get a Covid test here in Puebla?" Cassie looked thoughtful, but hope radiated from her slight smile.

"That I will investigate today, I hope. Then, we still have to get tickets somehow."

"Many things to conquer, I see," Maria nodded as she placed some strawberry jam on the table. "I could call my doctor's office to inquire about the test," she offered.

"That would be great, Mom. In the meantime, I will keep trying to get us earlier tickets. Also, let's see what the news has to say on T.V." I jumped up to turn the television onto the local news channel. I returned to my chair at the table, taking a bite of sausage, before glancing up at the word *confinamiento*, which means "lockdown" in Spanish. "What in the world? Did you hear that, Mom?"

Cassie stopped sipping her coffee, looking over to Luis. "What did they say?"

"Yes, I heard. This is very difficult news for the country."

"They are going into lockdown here, too, like in Oregon and Washington and in other places in the U.S. Let's listen to more before we get too worried." As the news disseminated, we learned that effective in three days, non-essential businesses, schools, churches, everything but essential to life things such as food or medicines, or household items, would be on lockdown. No one would be allowed to enter hospitals except for the staff and patients there. People in offices would work from home, so Maria supposed that Esteban would soon be doing that as well.

Chapter 15

Cassie

*"Let the rain kiss you. Let the rain beat upon
your head with silver liquid drops.
Let the rain sing you a lullaby."*

—*Langston Hughes*

The wind pelted the rain at the windows; I listened with contentment and watched as Abbie looked out. "Mommy, can we go outside and feel the rain drops? Please?" She stared at me longingly, pawing at the window with her fingertips, smearing the condensation, attempting to touch the drops from within the house.

"No, little one. It' a storm. We have to wait until it lets up a little." I kissed the top of Abbie's frizzy hair, grinning at its texture, so like mine. She was a part of me, with my father's African American heritage. Such an exotic but lovely blend, our Abbie. My mother was white, and Luis, of course, is Hispanic. I will have to protect her. She will be up against bullies in school, I imagine. I reached out to hug her, to shield her from the future.

"What, Mommy? When can we go outside?"

"Soon enough, little one. Here, I'll crack the window a fraction to *breathe in the rain-washed air." I breathed in deeply, hugging Abbie once more, experiencing the sensation together.*

Just at that moment, I felt something or someone shaking my shoulder. "Wake up, Cassie. You're dreaming again." Luis' face was bent close to mine.

"No! Not again! I don't want to wake up yet. Let me have this dream." But it had evaporated with his voice; I was fully alert. Regretfully, I opened my eyes.

"Come on and get up. We're going to take a bus to the U.S. Consulate today, remember?" Luis pulled at my arm, forcing me to sit up.

"Oh, right. Okay. Give me a minute," I said, rubbing at my eyes, my body slowly awakening. It was such a sweet dream, too. I stumbled into the bathroom, splashing water on my face, and brushing my teeth. I was careful to use bottled water for my teeth. I didn't want to risk getting sick with the water that came out of the faucet.

"So, are Tully, Claire, and all the gang coming with us?"

"Not sure. Why don't you call them and see what they decided?"

"I will. But first, coffee please." Sluggishly, I ambled down to the kitchen where I smelled coffee already. I sucked in the aroma, willing it to commence the wake-up process.

Eventually, we were able to get through on the hotel line and checked in with Tully. No one was up as far as she knew, so we said we would let them know whatever we found out at the consulate later. Luis wanted to get going while it was early in the day, before the people at the consulate left for lunch.

"What exactly, are we going to ask about there? I thought you found out that it was possible to return to the U.S." We had boarded the bus, masked up, and Luis had difficulty understanding what I had said. The bus jerked and bumped, and we hung on, since no seats were available. I nearly lost my footing as the bus swayed to a stop.

"Let's talk after we get off," Luis suggested, and I nodded in agreement.

WE STOOD IN LINE FOR NEARLY AN HOUR BEFORE BEING ABLE to speak to someone at the Consulate. I felt like I was at the DMV back in the States. As Luis explained our situation, reverting at times to Spanish, the representative merely nodded, saying very little until Luis ended his long narrative of our predicament. The woman over the counter put on the appropriate sympathetic face before launching into her answer. "So, you see, there are many U.S. citizens seeking to leave. We cannot guarantee when you will be able to depart Mexico." Her smile was a thin line, as she bent over our paperwork which Luis had filled out during our hour wait. "Plus, we too, just heard that Mexico is going into lockdown in a few days. That may change things as well. However," she hurried to add, noting the dejected look on our faces, "we will surely try to expedite your request. For now, what you must do is comply with the lockdown here and wait for us to call to let you know that we have secured tickets for your return."

"Thank you. We appreciate anything that you can do for us—and for our friends and Casandra's mother, who is also here in Mexico."

"Well, I'm not sure we can do much for that many people, but your request, with your small child alone in the U.S., will receive attention. That is all." With that, the woman turned her head to look behind us in the line, proclaiming, "Next" in a loud voice. Luis picked up the receipt for the paperwork he turned in, and we slowly made our way out to the street.

Chapter 16

CASSIE

"So, Mom, tell Claire and Preston and Tommy that we visited the U.S. Consulate today. Not great news but it could be positive for Luis and me. They will try to get us out to get back to Abbie. They said everyone wants to get back home but with the lockdown, they aren't sure how many will be able to." I heard the pause, the steady breathing over the phone.

Tully hesitated before responding to my news. "Okay. I suppose we all have to make the best of it here. We can at least take walks around the city, right?" Tully chuckled a bit—a forced attempt at levity.

"Right. Let's all take a walk later today and mull this over. I'm still in shock at how things are going."

We all met up in the downtown area of the city after lunch and strolled down the sidewalk, pausing to peer into closed stores and shops. Preston and Claire took the lead, and the rest of us paired off as it were, with Tommy and Viviana, Luis with me, and Tully and Robert, all trailing behind Preston and Claire aimlessly. Mercedes attached herself close to Viviana's side as usual. We came to the city square where benches afforded a place to sit down. "So, what do you think? How long will our finances hold out to pay for hotel rooms? How long before we can go home?" Claire voiced what all were thinking.

"Well," Tully answered, "I'm thinking that we should consider getting a short-term apartment together. It's perhaps cheaper than our total cost of hotel rooms, right?" She glanced over at Luis for his opinion. After all, he was from Puebla, even though it had been several years since he lived there.

It was Viviana who answered. She lived in Puebla presently and had first-hand information on rents and pricing. "Well, I would say yes, it's cheaper and better to have a small apartment rather than all of you forking over hotel room pricing. I know a friend who rents out apartments for a living. I could check with her to see if there might be an affordable place for all of you to hang out for a while. It would need to be furnished, of course."

At that, Tommy squeezed her hand affectionately. He placed a kiss on her forehead, saying, "Thank you, Viv, from all of us." He rarely showed his feelings in groups and Viviana looked over at him, and leaned in, her head touching his shoulder.

"Selfishly, I hope you can stay for a time here in Puebla," she whispered. "I don't want you to leave, Tommy."

"Well, yes, that's an idea," Luis replied. "I was thinking about that possibility for all of you. I wish my folks could put you all up, but there are too many of you, with Preston, Claire, Tully, Robert, and Tommy. "Perhaps you could begin searching but take a little time to see if the airlines might open up for you to all return home. What do the rest of you think?"

"Okay, but how do we do this search? Will you help us? We don't know the language, you know," Preston chided good naturedly.

"But of course, Viv, Mercedes, and I will help with this." Luis chuckled, grabbing my hand as we all sat and contemplated our plight. A pigeon pecked by my feet; I stared at it absently, wishing

Linda L. Graham

suddenly that Abbie was there to watch the bird. She would squeal in delight. Soon, other pigeons appeared to join in the search for crumbs.

"Yes, let me check with my friend. I'm sure we can find you all something suitable." Out of the side of my vision, I observed Tommy giving Viviana a peck on the cheek. She nuzzled closer to him on the bench and took his hand.

Robert sat, obviously deep in thought like the rest of us. He glanced over to Tully. "So, I already live in Mexico up in the Monarch Sanctuary. I should be able to get back there by bus anytime I wish. Of course, Tully, you might want to join me there while you wait for a flight out of the country. What do you think, Tully?" He put his arm around her and pulled her close.

"Uh, oh, I don't know. This is all so sudden. Let me think about that idea." Nervously, she cleared her throat. Her mind raced, considering the possibility but also what it implied—staying on a mountain top with Robert, alone.

"Sure, sure. Just another option to consider. I could also stay here with you while this plays out." Robert stood up abruptly, shuffling around behind the benches. The pigeons scattered with his movement and flew off.

Chapter 17

CASSIE

*"I need the seasons to live to
the rhythm of rain and sun."*

—Sophie Marcean

The next morning, I reached over to hold Abbie close, and then realized with a terrible jolt that I was only dreaming again. There was no one next to me after all—not even Luis. He had already gone downstairs. I could smell the coffee wafting up the stairs. Then I heard his footsteps, nearly running as he mounted the stairs two at a time. He threw open the door, which was already ajar, and entered, grinning widely. "Cass, I have some good news! The U.S. Consulate called. They are arranging for you and me to fly back home in three days!" He took hold of my arm, shaking me. "Sit up, Cassie. Shake the cobwebs from your brain. We can go back to see our baby girl!"

"Huh—what are you saying? That can't be. I think I'm still dreaming." I slid back down onto my pillow and brought the covers over my shoulders. "Let me just sleep a little more, Luis."

"No, no! It's true! We can make plans to leave in just three days, Sweetie. The consulate told me that. We have an itinerary. Here, I'll show you on my phone." Luis bent down to show the flight itinerary, but I just couldn't comprehend it yet. It was a dream come true, but I had had too many disappointing dreams lately.

"Okay, let me get up and splash water on my face, get some coffee, and then I will look at your phone."

When we broke the news to the rest of our group, tears gathered at the edges of Tully's eyes. Claire smiled for our joy, but I saw the disappointment behind it. Everyone had hoped to go home, but it was only to be for Luis and me. These were not fun times to be locked down in a third world country. I knew what they were all fearing—the dreaded virus—having to be hospitalized here and hoping to live through it far away from home. "I'm so happy for you, dear," Tully said. Claire nodded in agreement.

"Surely, they will relent, and let you all return soon. They have to!" I proclaimed, trying to sound optimistic. Our group had gathered at our new spot, in the town square, all of us occupying the two benches afforded there.

"Preston and I must get back to our jobs. What will happen to our jobs while we are here, I don't know. It's a worry."

Preston's gaze looked despondent. "Right. I was hoping to get home now, too. Such a setback."

Silently, I noticed that Tommy and Viviana, holding hands, looked smugly content. He could stay with her a while longer. Robert, too, appeared at peace, and reached over to touch Tully's shoulder, smiling down into her face. "Tully, have you given it any more thought as to joining me at the Monarch Sanctuary? I think I'll leave in two more days. I have some research to attend to up there."

Nervously, Tully looked down at her feet. "Well, I am still thinking about it. I'll let you know what I decide before you leave, okay?"

"You should go, Tully. What a nice offer. And you'll be with Robert," Claire grinned knowingly.

"I—I know. Just not sure yet."

"It does get a bit lonely up there by myself. Just my dog and me. It would be nice to finally have some company." Robert took his arm down from Tully's shoulder to grasp her hand tightly. "But no pressure."

Tully glanced over to Robert, relief in her face. "Sure. I appreciate that. Again, I'll let you know."

"Say, I saw a street vendor selling tacos. Let's get some lunch, alright?" Luis was eager to change the topic.

"Good idea. I'm starved!" Preston agreed, and everyone jumped up to walk across the way to where they knew the taco guy would be.

Luis and I caught the bus back to his parents' in time for dinner. Later, as I crawled into bed, I went over the events of the day. For the first time since the pandemic broke out, I felt happy—excited even. I snuggled under the covers and sighed. I could return home to my baby Abbie in just three days! As I drifted off in slumber, my dreams were there, waiting for me. I was holding Abbie in my arms, her head close to my nose. I could smell her baby innocence…and drifted into bliss.

Chapter 18
CASSIE

"Most of my memories are the sound of rain on caravan roofs."

—Kelly Macdonald

It hit me like an iron skillet over the head: excruciating headache, fever, chills, nausea, but worst of all, a gut wrenching, persistent cough wracked my diaphragm and up through my throat. It was three in the morning. I moaned in pain. Instantly, Luis was awake, leaning over, his head close to mine. "Cassie, are you okay?"

"No—I feel awful," I croaked. Just at that moment, I knew I was going to throw up, and I leaped out of bed to stagger down the hall to the bathroom. I made it just in time, but also had diarrhea at the same moment as vomiting. Along with the hacking cough. All at the same time. Horrific. *This was Covid*, I realized.

"Cass, are you okay?" Luis knocked on the bathroom door. "May I come in?" Barging in, he saw me in all my horrid glory. "Here, let me help you clean up and then you get into bed. I'll bring you some water and hot tea. First, though, let me get Mom's thermometer and take your temperature."

I was too shaky to argue. The cough attacked with a vengeance—my eyes felt like they would pop out of my head. Wobbling and coughing, I made it back to the bed and Luis came in with the thermometer. Indeed, I had a temperature of 102 degrees Fahrenheit.

These were the early days of the virus, and no home testing existed. However, since Luis was a medical doctor, he was able to obtain a testing kit and came back to test me. I tested positive for Covid. Our return tickets home to Abbie in two days were canceled. Sadly, I lay there in bed, coughing, feeling miserable, and not eating. I had no appetite—no taste. The crackers and toast that were offered tasted like sawdust in my mouth. Luis insisted that I stay hydrated, so I managed to down a little water or tea.

Luis intercepted the calls from Tully and our friends, relaying the news of the virus. I isolated in the bedroom, trying to quarantine from the rest of the family, but Luis, of course, was exposed. He wore a mask each time he was around me, as well as around the family. Everyone in the household masked up, fearing they would come down with the illness. As I lay in a fever, hacking my guts out, I tried not to become too dejected at not going home to Abbie. I was just too sick to truly care at that point.

Luis attempted to entice me with food of any kind, but I wasn't having it. I lay there, barely drinking tea and water, for three days. I lost weight, but my fever didn't let up. On the fourth day, my fever had risen to 104 degrees. Also on that fourth day, I was struggling to breathe. Luis gathered me up, wrapped me in a blanket, and stuffed me into a cab bound for the hospital. I was near delirium, but managed to hear his commanding voice as we entered emergency, with him carrying me in his arms. "Get my wife a wheelchair, and take her to the I.C.U. She can't breathe—Covid!" I saw him flash his medical identification from the U.S. The nurse didn't argue. A wheelchair appeared, and I was whisked down the hall. Luis followed in hot pursuit.

My memory from that point is a blur. Luis told me later that I was placed on a ventilator which stayed on for a week. I was fed intravenously. Needless to say, we missed the three-day window to use our new tickets to return home.

As I lay breathing on the ventilator, my mind going in and out of consciousness, I visualized my Abbie. *"Watch, Mommie!" Abbie stuck out her tongue to catch the rain drops. Her hair glistened with the clean, cleansing moisture of rain. The towering fir trees gently swayed with the breeze, their massive branches whispering their approval. The trees formed a natural dome, a cathedral to the heavens, as I raised my head to see their perfect symmetry, offering an opening to view the sky overhead. Abbie laughed as she captured each drop on her tongue, her face wet with nature's tears.* The snippets of life in the majestic Northwest always entered my subconscious, as I longed for home.

I moaned, reaching out my hand to touch my daughter's soft, rain drenched, hair. I touched the crisp sheets on my bed instead.

Chapter 19

LUIS

*M*y wife, Cassie, has Covid and is in intensive care on a ventilator. I so feared that there wouldn't be one for her, but I insisted. I know a local physician from medical school. He made sure he could get her connected on one. I'm worried sick that she won't pull through; I need her—Abbie needs her. We all do. My life will be nothing if she doesn't live through this horrible virus. I remain by her side at the hospital twenty-four hours a day, checking her vitals, making sure she gets the best possible care here. I see that others in here are not allowed visitors, due to the virus, but they know I'm a doctor, and allow me to stay. I have to. That is what I trained for, and she is my life—my love.

I sat, my eyes fixed on Cassie and her monitors, listening to her breathing through the ventilator. I was exhausted beyond reason but more afraid than I had ever been in my life. *What if she doesn't make it? To die here in Mexico, away from the life she knows, away from sweet Abbie, our baby girl. What kind of justice is that, God? Please, God. Let her live.* I bowed his head and sobbed.

Chapter 20

Cassie

A week to the day that I had been placed on a ventilator, Luis also came down with Covid. He stayed at the hospital in my room non-stop, even showering in my bathroom there, and taking meals in the hospital. But now he too, was very ill. He was able to accompany me back to his parents' home but took to the sick bed there in the bedroom we were sharing. "Cassie, I prayed that you would live while we were there in the hospital. You may have to pray for me, now," he said, smiling weakly. "I guess we are both quarantined here in this room for a while."

"Of course, Luis. I'm just glad we are together. We'll get through it."

Maria left our meals and essentials outside the door to our room. We only left the room to use the bathroom down the hall. Hopefully, no one else in the family would contract the disease. All we could do was to take precautions, wear a mask when we left the room, and hope. And pray.

Luis became very sick as well but seemed to have no difficulty breathing. His fever hovered around 102 degrees, and then lessoned. On the fifth day, he seemed a tiny bit better, and even smiled at me as I adjusted his covers. "Cass, I think I'll make it." His grin looked a little like his old self, and I took heart.

"Okay, I agree. You'll be well in no time, now."

"Well, I don't know about that," he said, in between coughing spells, "but perhaps."

In actuality, we were both in small steps of recovery. We had a long way to go. I became winded just walking down the hall to the bathroom. I continued to have no taste or smell. Still, we were both lucky to be alive, and hoped that one day soon, we could try to get return tickets back to the states.

After Luis reached the ten-day mark, we ended our isolation. We still masked up in the house, hoping against hope that no one else would come down with it.

It wasn't to be. Before Luis' ten-day period ended, Maria began coughing and contracted a fever. She too, took to her sick bed, and the horrid cycle began once more in the house. This time, however, there was even more fear—Maria was older. We knew that older people didn't fare so well. After just three days, Luis took her to the emergency room as well. As he left with her, I saw his set features—he was terribly concerned. The eyes above his mask told me everything I needed to know. He was worried for her life.

Later that evening, he called from the hospital. "Cass, I'm so scared for Mom. She's in intensive care now, and on a ventilator. Cass—," his voice broke. He couldn't continue. "I—I feel so helpless. Nothing I can do medically. Just wait by her side."

"It's alright, Luis. It's not your fault this happened. We did our best to keep the family well by isolating. It's going to be okay. We are all praying for her."

"I called Dad already. He wants to see her, but no visitors allowed, you know."

It occurred to me after we hung up that once more our departure plans would be delayed. Even our original itinerary departure date had elapsed. We had already been away from home and Abbie for three weeks, and now there was no end in sight yet. We had to see Maria's illness through. Once more, we were stuck here in Mexico. I, too, was worried for Maria—leaving here was out of the question. In my mind, I pictured little Abbie, reaching out and calling for me.

Chapter 21

TULLY

I finally gave in and took a bus from Puebla to the Monarch Sanctuary to join Robert. Why not? None of us can get our flight back home yet, so I might as well tour around up there with him and enjoy myself. He really is nice to be around. I think I might be attracted to him, but we will see how it goes. We haven't had much time together at one stretch, so this will be interesting to see where our relationship goes. I'm almost there now, and Robert is to meet me in Angangueo, the small village where we all stayed before. Robert will descend the mountain on horseback to greet me in front of the hotel there.

Suddenly, the bus arrived, and all the passengers deboarded—there were six of us. As I stepped off, there he was, smiling, with his arms crossed. He was more handsome than I remembered last. I saw him just ten days ago, in Puebla, but that was with all our group. Now it was just the two of us. Nervously, I bent down to pick up my bag. Before I could get hold of it, Robert was there, grabbing it for me.

"Welcome back to the mountain, Tully!" He beamed at me and bent over to give me a peck on the cheek.

I didn't know how to respond. I felt like a schoolgirl again and giggled.

"Uh, hello, Robert. I made it."

"Yes, you did." I had to walk fast to keep up with him as he led the way to the stable. We had to ride horseback to his cabin which was located at the summit. "So, did you bring a small bag to take for one night or so until the supply truck makes it up in a couple of days with your large one?" He glanced down at my big piece of luggage he was carrying.

"Y-yes. I have this to bring for now," I answered, motioning to the backpack I had slung over my shoulder. I felt so awkward, like I had never gone off on an adventure with a man before. Actually, I hadn't. I was so naïve for a middle-aged woman. I had married young, and then eventually divorced. I had one brief fling, but it was nothing like going to an isolated cabin with a man. I realized that now and felt even more apprehensive than ever. Robert was sure to pick up on my hesitance.

"It's okay to feel a bit weird about this. I am, too, actually. I've never had company to stay overnight at my cabin," he said, laughing nervously. "Well, except for Jose and his mother, Cecilia. Very much alone up there, except for my dog."

"Oh, right. The dog. What's his name again?" At least, something to talk about besides our going to a cabin alone together.

"Bogey. He's not only a great companion, but also a good watch dog. No one else to help me if something happened, or an intruder came." He noticed my stricken look at the word 'intruder'. "No worries. Nothing has ever happened up there. Very peaceful."

"Uh, what kind of dog is Bogey?" I asked, grateful to keep my mind off what lay ahead.

"Oh, mostly a mutt, but kind of like a Golden Retriever. Maybe some Lab, a large dog."

"Okay. Gentle, I hope?"

At that, Robert chuckled. "Well, he is a good watchdog. That's what I want up there. He won't hurt you, don't worry.".

We arrived at the stable, where Jose awaited, three horses saddled and ready for the journey. We mounted and set off. I rode a pinto named Candy, while Robert was riding a tall, dapple-grey called Smokey. Jose rarely looked back at us as the horses plodded up the hillside. The horses knew the way well; they carried tourists to the Monarch Sanctuary daily. For some reason on this day, we were the only ones.

In about two hours, we reached the summit. The horses knew it was time to stop and enjoy nibbling grass. As I glanced around before dismounting, I noticed a few Monarch butterflies lazily circling in the sky overhead. The cabin lay about a hundred yards from us; it looked inviting but also lonely—very isolated. *What was I thinking?*

"Come on, Tully. I'll show you my castle. Get you settled in." Robert took my hand and helped me dismount from Candy. Candy snorted, and then resumed her delicate biting off grass blades. My legs were wobbly from the long ride, I presumed, but perhaps there was more to it. Tentatively, I plodded across the grass to the steps of the cabin. Robert gripped my elbow and assisted me up each step. He waved farewell to Jose, who had been instructed to just return down the trail with all three horses. My main luggage was to arrive tomorrow, hopefully, by the supply truck. There was a dirt road for vehicles to the top as well. I drew a deep breath and stepped across the threshold.

My breath caught as I saw the table, set for two, with a fresh bouquet of mountain flowers in the middle. A bottle of wine, a cabernet, was poised near the flowers, along with two wine glasses. "Everything looks just lovely, Robert," I commented, turning to smile into his face, which at that moment, was very close to mine.

"Thank you, Tully. I want you to feel at home." Just then, he took me in his arms, and kissed my lips. I felt a bit awkward again, taking all of this in as a cue from him that we might become intimate up here, alone. I wasn't sure I was ready yet, but here I was, miles up a mountain, alone with Robert. I had agreed to come.

"Come. I'll show you my loft bedroom. Just take a peek. I bought a new comforter," he added, grinning sheepishly. Nervously, I followed him up the rickety steps to the loft. As I entered, I observed yet more flowers on the nightstand. The comforter, in muted shades of blue, beckoned invitingly. I suddenly realized that I was exhausted from the long journey. The bed looked so cozy, imploring me to take a nap. "So, where will you sleep?" I asked, teasing, yet a little seriously at the same time.

"Oh—well—I can make up the sofa to sleep on. No problem," he quickly added, taking my jesting in stride. "Let's have dinner. I bought a couple of steaks while in town. Salad is already made." Robert led the way down the rickety steps back to the main floor and into the kitchen. I followed him down carefully, rethinking my decision to come here.

As it happened, Robert didn't need to make up the sofa. We drank the wine plus some champagne he had on hand, along with eating a delicious dinner. We talked and laughed, and then relaxed on the sofa, sipping the champagne from fluted glasses, and watching the fire in the fireplace. The flames crackled, sending a few sparks up the chimney. Robert and I watched the fire silently for a few minutes. Soon, we were in one another's arms and eventually he gently carried me up to the loft. Robert never needed to make up the sofa.

Chapter 22

CASSIE

Maria had been hanging on in the I.C.U. for the last two weeks but wasn't out of danger yet. It was hard to think of anything else, even though I missed my Abbie terribly. She would just have to get by without me a while longer. I tried to call her and Jasmine daily but didn't always get through. Occasionally, I thought about my adopted mom suddenly taking off to meet up with Robert at the Monarch Sanctuary; however, I couldn't let my mind worry about her too. After all, she could take care of herself, I reasoned. *Funny, she is with my biological father, Robert.* Crazy how life takes unexpected twists.

I awaited Luis' return from the hospital to hear the update on Maria. We all hoped and prayed for her to take a turn for the better. I went downstairs to make coffee, when I found Viviana in the kitchen, coffee already made. "Here have a cup," she motioned, pouring some coffee into a mug. Without a word, I took the proffered cup and sat down. Viviana followed me to the table and sat across from me. Silently, we sipped, although the liquid was a bit too hot. "So, do you think my mom is going to make it?"

Her eyes met mine over our mugs. I noticed that hers were red rimmed, either from no sleep or crying or both. For the first time,

I thought about how all of this must be affecting Luis' whole family. I was so preoccupied in my own misery of losing my grandpa and being away from Abbie. I scolded myself, thinking how self-centered I had been. "Well, to tell the truth, I'm not too sure. Covid is a harsh illness, especially for older people." I looked down into my cup, avoiding her intense gaze.

"Well, I know. And I'm so sorry about your grandfather. I don't think I ever told you that." She reached out across the table to touch my free hand.

"Thank you. We have to hope and pray for Maria now." Just then, Mercedes padded into the kitchen to get a cup of coffee and sat down with us. It was obvious that she, too, had been crying already. I realized then that I needed to help support these two, as well as Luis and Esteban. They were going through a lot right now. "Hey, Mercedes. Sit down with us. Hopefully, Luis will get back soon with some good news."

I had heard earlier from Mercedes that Tommy and Viviana were spending a lot of time together now. In fact, every day they were getting together, no matter that the city was in lockdown. Even so, I still wasn't prepared for the news: Viviana was pregnant.

I just had to ask Luis about it, although I hated to bother him during the stressful time of his mother's illness. "Well, you know. Nature will take its course sometimes," he replied, chuckling. I thought he would be outraged. Instead, he thought it was all a natural development.

"Okay, but how will your father react when he gets the news?"

"Hopefully, he won't hear about this for a while. Mom's condition is still on the line." Luis gave me a warning look.

"Of course! Don't look at me like that. I won't be the one to tell him. Don't worry."

"Guess I better head it off by telling Viv and Mercedes not to say anything yet. One crisis at a time."

Luis, Mercedes, Viviana, and I met up with the rest of the group at their new apartment. It was just Claire, Preston, and Tommy who were living in the tiny apartment, located closer to the downtown area. We took the bus to get there, masked as usual. I noticed that Tommy avoided Viviana's eyes as we filed in and sat down at their kitchen table. It was a good thing I was still wearing my mask, since I was smirking underneath it. *Well, well, well. Little secret, have we?*"

"Okay, group. Where shall we walk today?" Claire looked around, waiting for a response.

"I still don't know my way around everything here. What do you say, Luis?" Preston looked over to Luis for an answer.

"Well, you've been there before, but how about walking through the area by city hall and then stop by the cathedral. I want to pray for Mom."

"Sure. Let's go." Preston grabbed Claire's hand, and we set off. Luis took my hand in his, as did Tommy with Viviana's. Mercedes kept up the pace beside her sister. As we neared the vicinity of the city hall buildings, it was very apparent that they were locked shut. Few people were out on the street except for us. The city was certainly on lockdown.

"I totally forgot that the cathedral would also be closed due to lockdown. I guess I'll have to do my prayer outside on a nearby bench."

"That's okay, Luis. We'll go with you," Claire assured him. We all meandered over to the nearest bench to the cathedral and sat down. Luis made the sign of the cross and silently prayed. One by one we either prayed silently, or at least gave quiet respect until all were finished. After a few minutes, we rose as one, and silently moved on. We walked for at least another mile, mostly in ruminative silence. As we neared a park with trees, Tommy and Viviana exchanged glances, and she nodded.

"Could we find another bench or two and sit awhile? Viviana and I have something to tell you." Tommy appeared nervous, but Viviana squeezed his hand, seeming to assure him.

"Sure, Tommy. Let's sit over here," Preston said, motioning to a set of benches under a tree. All that we could hear were birds singing above. We all sat down, glad for a break in the constant walking. No one said much. We just enjoyed the shade of the tree, and the quiet of the park.

"Well, group, I guess Viviana and I need a little advice. You see…." his voice wavered. "You see, it's like this. Viviana and I love each other. We wanted to ask her parents about us getting married someday. When churches are open again. Now her mother is in I.C.U. And, more than that," Tommy broke off, unable to continue.

"What Tommy wants to say is that I'm pregnant." Viviana stared at her feet, her face reddening a bit.

"Oh! I didn't know!" Claire gasped, a bit surprised.

"Me either, but hey! It's okay, right?" Preston asked.

"Mercedes told us," I confessed, looking at Luis, who nodded.

"We are sworn to secrecy, until you tell Dad," Luis added quickly.

"So, what do we do now? There are no weddings, due to lockdown, and Mom's in the hospital, so Dad is worried sick for her." Viviana started crying, but Tommy took her hand and put his arm around her for support.

"And the baby to come?" Claire asked the question gently, insinuating more than she stated.

"Of course—I intend to keep the baby. It will be viewed as a blessing by my parents, regardless." Viviana wiped at her tears with the back of her free hand. Tommy was nodding vigorously.

"We had just hoped to marry soon, but now? What can we do? How long will the lockdown continue?" Tommy looked at each of us for answers. We had none.

"We'll help you find a way," I finally said, trying to smile hopefully.

Chapter 23

CASSIE

Another week dragged by, with Maria just barely surviving, and still on a ventilator. Luis became more withdrawn, the worry creasing his brows, and he ate very little. He visited the hospital daily and brought home any updates. Esteban, too, seemed distracted with concern. Viviana and Mercedes tried to fill Maria's void, cooking and cleaning with a vengeance. Tommy dropped by to see Viviana, but she only gave him a tight smile and hug. I was overcome with anxiety for Maria and all of them. After all, I knew how it went with my grandfather. Our group included walks to the cathedral at least once a week. We joined Luis on the bench while he prayed outside the building.

Yesterday, Viviana and Mercedes headed out, not saying where they were going. Luis and I watched them leave, curious. "Where do you suppose they are going?"

"I have no idea," Luis answered. "I'm wondering as well. Perhaps they will tell us when they get back." Sure enough, later that day, they pulled us aside.

"So, we went, along with Tommy, and spoke with our priest, outside the chapel. We explained the situation with Viv and Tommy wanting to be married. We're working on a way to hold a wedding in the church gardens." Mercedes looked excited to reveal the news.

Viviana's eyes danced, adding, "But we must talk to Dad first. That's the scary part. Plus, we are still worried about Mom. What do you think?"

"That's a novel idea, no doubt. What about Mom? She will miss out," Luis reminded her.

"Yes, I thought about that. Maybe we could just have a very small wedding of family and a few friends, and then have a larger one when she returns home, and this lockdown is over."

"That's all good, but what about telling Dad? I'm not sure how he will take this. He's pretty old fashioned, you realize."

Viviana drew in a quick breath. "I—I know. Not sure yet how to break the news of the baby to him. Plus, you know, Tommy is a U.S. citizen, as well as Asian." Her eyes spoke of the worry.

"Well, Dad took to Cassie just fine. Perhaps it won't be such a big deal as you imagine. I'll think on it and get back to you on how and when to say something."

Viviana smiled gratefully. "Thank you, big brother."

"Yeah, thanks, man," Tommy added.

A WEEK WENT BY WITH LUIS SAYING NOTHING TO THE COUPLE. Finally, he took them aside during our daily walk around with the group. We were admiring the trees in a city park. I missed the foliage of the Northwest, but at least, there were a few trees here in this Puebla city park. "So, I spoke with Dad. I just laid it out for you to soften him up before you speak to him. Maybe you should do that either today or tomorrow." Luis grinned at Tommy; eyebrows arched. "You know, before he has a chance to reconsider."

"Reconsider? What do you mean?" Viviana asked.

"Well, he just said he could live with the idea of a quick wedding, if you have a nice one once Mom is back home. He took it pretty well, all things considered."

"That's great! I'll speak to him and ask for her hand right away." Tommy suddenly felt energized, confident to confront Viviana's father—now that Luis had paved the way. Tommy grabbed Viviana's hand, almost in a symbolic gesture for what was to come. They smiled into one another's eyes. All would be well—at least for now.

Esteban didn't make the conversation with Tommy very easy. Viviana and Tommy sat on the sofa, holding hands. Esteban sat across from them on a straight back chair, glowering at them, awaiting the conversation to commence. Viviana toyed with her hair nervously. "Um, Mr. Mendez, I have something important to discuss with you." Tommy couldn't meet Esteban's gaze. "It, uh, actually involves Viviana." Esteban stared across from Tommy, his face a blank, as if he couldn't imagine where the conversation was headed.

"Oh? What could you want to talk about, Tommy? Are you still enjoying your visit to Puebla?"

"Well, er, yes. It's quite nice here, even with the lockdown, sir. But actually—"

"Dad, I'm pregnant," Viviana broke in abruptly, hoping to make things easier.

"Pregnant? How did that happen?" Esteban asked playfully. He tried to suppress a grin but was unsuccessful.

"Well, sir, uh, I love your daughter very much. I—I want to ask you if we could be married soon." Tommy wiped his forehead, a sweat of nervousness breaking out. "Just a small ceremony of close friends and family. Later, perhaps we could hold a larger one, like a renewal, when this lockdown is over."

"And Mom is back home to help me to plan a proper wedding," Viviana interjected again.

"Hmm." Esteban rubbed his chin thoughtfully. "How old are you, Tommy?"

Tommy sat up straighter, looking Esteban squarely in the eye. "I'll be thirty next month, sir. I'm old enough to care for Viviana and a child, I believe. Sir."

"Well, yes. I should think so. However, I'm not sure what you can do here in Mexico to earn a living with so few Spanish language skills. But, Viviana, what do you feel for this young man?" Esteban shifted his gaze to her, continuing to rub his chin.

"Oh, Daddy, I love this man. Please give us your blessing." She looked down at her hands, nervously waiting for his reply.

"All right, then. You may have your quick ceremony, if it is with a priest, and then you plan a renewal of vows or a reception at a later time. Your mother will want a large reception. One issue I'm worried about is how you will handle the difference in citizenship. I'm not sure how Tommy can provide for you here. Possibly, we could use an additional office clerk where I work at City Hall. I will check into that.

Relief flooded Viviana's face. Yes, Dad. We will work on the citizenship issue. Thank you so much. We talked to our priest already. He is willing to do the wedding outdoors."

"Thank you, Mr. Mendez. I will take good care of her, don't worry, Sir."

"Call me Esteban. Mr. Mendez is too formal for family." He grinned good naturedly.

"Yes, Mr., uh, Esteban. Thank you."

Love finds a way, I suppose. With Tommy being able to speak very limited Spanish, his job prospects in Mexico would be difficult. It might be easier to have Viviana apply for residency in the U. S. over time, after she married Tommy. Many hurdles loomed ahead to figure out. In the meantime, Maria still lay in the hospital, suffering with Covid.

Chapter 24

CASSIE

The wedding took place the following week. Viviana wore a simple, full-length dress in soft pink crepe with an empire waist and carried a small bouquet of pink tea roses. She was already getting a baby bump, so the dress was gathered above the waist and fell in full folds of fabric. Her long glossy black hair was swept into a modest French braid, interwoven with pink ribbon. Her father, Esteban, escorted her up to the makeshift altar area where a table, holding a candle, had been placed. A vase containing a bouquet of assorted flowers in shades of pink and white adorned the table as well. The priest, along with Tommy and his best man, Preston, awaited them. Mercedes, maid of honor, also took her place close to the altar after preceding Esteban and Viviana down the sidewalk. Mercedes wore a lime green street length dress and carried a small bouquet of pink tea roses to match Viviana's bouquet. Her hair was also arranged in a French braid, and there was no mistaking her as Viviana's sister—they could have passed for twins. As Viviana and Esteban approached, she smiled shyly, looking into Tommy's eyes. He was dressed in black slacks with a classic white shirt, a tea rose pinned to it, and wore a tie in rose-colored stripes. As a soft breeze stirred Viviana's hair from the tendrils around her face, she approached her groom, radiant and blushing.

The day was overcast and cool; we all stood silently outside the church in the garden area, some of us shivering, while the priest officiated the short ceremony. There were no chairs to sit. We could catch a whiff of bougainvillea, which was in full bloom in the garden. Overhead, in the trees, we heard birds singing, who provided the only music for the wedding. A breeze caught in the tree branches, gently swaying them, as if in unison with the birds' song. At that moment, both Claire and Mercedes dabbed their eyes with tissues. Mercedes blew her nose, and we all chuckled good naturedly. The only other sound was the priest, intoning the familiar solemn words, with Tommy and Viviana repeating them. It was all done in Spanish, but Tommy had memorized the vows, even though he didn't know the language well. I was close to tears but managed to hold it together as Luis and I stood together. Luis took my hand, as if in support, as we witnessed his sister being wed.

Afterward, we convened at the family home for sandwiches, cake, and champagne. Because of the lockdown, there was no honeymoon. The newly married couple simply rode a taxi to the apartment that Preston, Claire, and Tommy were renting. Viviana would move in with Tommy into his small bedroom, as life in lockdown continued.

I HAD HOPED THAT TULLY WOULD BE ABLE TO ATTEND THE last-minute wedding, but it was not to be. She was still up on the mountaintop of the Monarch Sanctuary with Robert. Due to lockdown precautions, all tours to the Sanctuary had been canceled, so there were few, if any, buses heading out of the mountainous region. So, she remained up there with Robert, as they researched and observed the butterflies together. Mostly Robert researched, but she was there to assist. I saw the humor and irony of that: she was my adoptive mother, and he, my biological father, working together, and falling in love, I supposed. Upon reflection, I realized that life was full of ironies. I was getting old enough to see it taking place in unexpected situations.

Chapter 25

Cassie

"Let us keep the dance of rain our fathers kept and tread our dreams beneath the jungle sky."
—Arnal Bontemps

"Mommy, I wish you were here. It's raining today. We could walk in the puddles and let the rain fall onto our tongues. I love to do that with you, Mommy. When are you coming home?" Abbie whined, sniffling as she talked.

My heart lurched. I wanted so much to share special moments with her. "Oh, Abbie, sweetie, I hope very soon. Ask Jasmine to take you outside to catch the rain on your tongue. Maybe she can. Ask her."

"I already did. She said she had to do laundry since she isn't teaching today. And she does this computer thing with the students at home but doesn't go anywhere. And Josh and Josie can't play with me either. They have to go to school on their computers all day."

Her comments brought a smile to my face. Abbie used such an adult word, "laundry". She was learning new things every day—and without me. That was the sad part. "I know, honey. Everyone must stay home to be safe right now. That's why I can't come home yet. Soon, we hope. You be good and do what Aunt Jasmine says, okay? Don't forget that I love you." At that point, the phone broke up, and I lost the connection. A sob caught in my throat; I wasn't sure if she heard that last part before I lost the phone connection. I hoped that she was cooperating with my sister and not creating too much extra stress on her. I had no way of knowing, however. Our calls were sketchy and short, just covering basic information with one another.

Life continued in hushed tones, with the lockdown hampering all our moves and decisions. Maria still hung on for her life in the hospital, so we didn't feel like we deserved to be happy or even to complain. I still only talked to Jasmine every week or so, and very rarely did I get to hear my little girl's voice. At least, today when I called, I did get to chat a bit with Abbie. I realized, sadly, that here I was down in Mexico while my Abbie was growing and changing every day. I was missing out on that.

Luis continued to go to the hospital daily to check on his mother. It was noon, and Mercedes and I were in the kitchen preparing a bite to eat when the house phone rang. Mercedes picked up, and I watched while she listened; her countenance grew serious. It was Luis. "Okay, Luis. We will be right over." Slowly, she hung up the phone, and her red eyes told the story." We have to get to the hospital right away. Mom isn't doing well. I'm calling Viviana and Dad so they can meet us there."

I used my cell phone to call a cab, and we rushed out in five minutes, locking the door behind us. It was a thirty-minute ride by taxi, and we ran to the entrance of the hospital, hoping that they would allow us inside. The door was locked, with a posted sign on the door informing us of no entry. As we waited there, Esteban showed up, and five minutes later, Viviana and Tommy arrived. Luis exited the hospital at last but shook his head. "They won't allow any of you to enter—sorry. I don't think she will make it beyond today. I'm so sorry." He lowered his head, trying to stifle the tears. His medical profession demeanor kept him from totally losing it. The sisters and Esteban embraced one another, and the tears let loose. Tommy and I just stood there, silently crying, but not knowing what to do, keeping our arms stiffly at our sides. We felt so helpless. This was the harsh reality of the pandemic. At least, Maria would have her son, Luis, present in her room to comfort her as she passed.

Maria departed this world two hours later. Luis phoned Mercedes when she passed. We all just waited for the call outside the hospital, praying for her to die in as little suffering as possible, and then, afterward, for her soul. There was nothing else we could do. Sadly, we slowly walked to catch a bus and returned as a group to the family home. There was to be no funeral, due to the pandemic. Esteban declared that there would be a funeral later on, after the lockdown was over. Everyone had to grieve in their own way, alone. Once more, the virus claimed another person, a loved one to many.

The wedding reception for Viviana and Tommy was also placed on permanent hold—cancelled. Now, there seemed to be no reason for celebration. There was no Maria. There was a baby on the way, due in six months. Still there was no word for Luis and me to return to our own little girl in the U.S. I longed to be home to see her as never before.

THE DAYS WORE ON ENDLESSLY IN PUEBLA. THE RELENTLESSLY hot, dry, dusty city reeking of stale food mixed with fuel stoked my desire to be rid of the place and return home. I dreamed of Abbie nightly, imagining the refreshing rains of the Great Northwest gently falling onto my face and hair. I had never realized until now how much I had taken the pristine ruggedness for granted. Now I understood that I had changed; I would forever be grateful once I was permitted to return to my majestic, green homeland. And Abbie.

My cell phone rang early one morning; I saw that it was Tully calling in. She didn't often get through since she was on the remote mountain top in the Monarch Sanctuary. Eagerly, I picked up. "Hi, Cassie. How is everything there in Puebla? Are you doing alright?"

"Oh, Mom. Wish you had been here. You heard that Maria passed away in the hospital, right?"

I heard nothing for a moment. Were we disconnected? "Oh, my gosh! We didn't know. Reception here is so sketchy. I'm so sorry!" Sadly, I filled in the details. She and Robert were enjoying their blissful existence up on the mountain and hadn't heard. My email never arrived. Tully promised to see if she could make it into Puebla soon. She would have to inquire if a tour bus could take her first into Mexico City and from there, wait for a bus going to Puebla. It would be a long journey and a bit uncertain due to the lockdowns.

The Mist

The towering trees rise from the mist,
Infusing the fragrance of sparkling rain.
Tree tops glisten with droplets
As a hawk soars above the firs,
Calling out its cry of joy of life—a brand new day.
The silence of the drizzle soaks into the fir needles
A carpet for the forest and all its inhabitants to trod.
As I look towards the heavens,
Nature's tears mingle with mine,
streaming down my cheeks,
Thankful for the privilege to live near this cleansing,
natural wonderland in the Northwest.

Linda L. Graham

Chapter 26

TULLY

"Tully, I'm thinking of asking Jose to bring up a couple of horses next time he conducts a tour group. I thought we could go into town to have lunch. I also want to show you something. What do you think? Do you have time to go?" Robert grinned, arching his eyebrows as he set down his coffee cup. We were sitting at the rustic wooden kitchen table sipping our morning coffee.

"Well, I suppose I could fit that into my busy schedule," I replied playfully, setting my cup down. "When did you have in mind? And what should I expect to see?"

"So many questions." Robert jumped up to refill our coffees. "I think Jose will be up here again tomorrow, so if I ask him when he arrives, he can bring us the horses in two more days. So, I was thinking, today is Monday, and he will be here Tuesday, so how about Thursday?"

"Well, all my days are the same up here, so sure! But I still want to know more about what we will see."

"Oh, well, my surprise. You'll see." His eyes twinkled. I had trouble with surprises, but I decided to let it go. I would find out soon enough.

On Tuesday, when Jose arrived with a small tour group, Robert walked over to where the group had hobbled their horses and were sitting on the grass eating sandwiches. Jose looked up as Robert strode purposefully straight to him. I sat on the chair on the cabin porch, observing. I wondered why the mystery. Robert asked if I would stay put while he spoke to Jose. Robert got close to Jose, sitting on his haunches while he talked in soft tones. The five tourists looked over, mildly curious, but neither man offered to explain why Robert lived there on the mountaintop. I wasn't able to catch the conversation, so I just continued to read a book.

Robert turned back to the cabin, smiling at me. As he mounted the steps, he finally spoke. "Okay, it's all set. We will get two horses to journey down the mountain on Thursday. Ready for a horseback ride?"

"Of course. That's how I got here, remember." I smiled, eagerly anticipating an exciting day on Thursday. It had been a while since we had been to the village of Angangueo, or anywhere else for that matter. I could not conceive of living in this cabin alone, year after year. How did he do it? No matter. I eagerly awaited our travel day to "civilization" in the small village.

When Thursday finally arrived, I dressed carefully for our luncheon date, even though we had to ride horseback for two hours before we would arrive. For this day, Jose chose an earlier guided excursion to accommodate Robert's request down the mountain. Jose and his tourists arrived promptly at ten o'clock. By ten thirty, everyone, including Robert and I, were headed down atop our assigned horses. We arrived at the village by 12:30, and Jose guided everyone into the stable area. We dismounted quickly, handing Jose the reins. "Thanks, Jose. See you later." I noticed that Robert gave Jose a meaningful stare but dismissed the thought; Robert headed towards the hotel for lunch in the dining room. Since the village was in a remote location, the lockdown for Covid did not seem to apply up here. The eatery in the hotel was still open to guests. I followed him from behind, my legs a bit wobbly from the horseback ride.

"Could you please slow down, Robert? My legs feel like rubber—I can barely walk."

"Oh, sure. Sorry. Guess I'm used to equine transportation," he said, chuckling and slowing to grab my hand. He swung my hand as we strolled, taking time now to reach the hotel. Ever so slowly, I mounted the steps.

Once seated, Robert nodded silently to the server, who set a table for three people. Next, the server brought out three menus. I looked around, my curiosity getting the most of me. "So, Robert, what's going on? Why did we come here today and what did you want to show me? And why is the table set for three?" I stared into his sable-colored eyes, which seemed to dance in anticipation.

"You will see very soon now. Just have a bit of patience." He smiled then, his eyes revealing nothing more. I was seated with my back to the doorway and didn't notice Jose until he arrived at the table. "There you are!" Robert exclaimed. "We've only been here a few minutes anyway."

"Sorry I was late. The tourists had questions I had to answer after we got back to the stable." Jose grabbed the chair where the third table setting was placed and sat down.

"Oh, hello, Jose. I didn't expect to see you here at the hotel. Did Robert invite you?" I felt confused and a bit taken back that Robert hadn't mentioned to me that he invited Jose to join them for lunch.

"Well, uh, yeah, he invited me," Jose replied, looking from me to Robert. Still, Robert stared with a blank expression, revealing nothing.

"So, this is unexpected. Are you bringing the mystery item that Robert promised to show me?" I grinned playfully, still perplexed, but decided to go along with the game. I toyed with my napkin, looking down at my hand and then up again, and waited.

Jose glanced over at Robert, who simply nodded. "Uh, yeah, I guess you could say that. Actually, uh, I'm the "mystery item". He chuckled nervously, hoping for Robert to say something.

"Yes, well, here it is: Tully, Jose is my son."

I let out a short gasp. "What are you saying? We just found out a few years back that Cassie is your daughter. Now this? How can that be?" I looked from Jose to Robert in bewilderment. Then, their physical similarities took shape in my mind. Even though Robert was African American, Jose did have some of his physical traits, along with a definite Hispanic appearance. His hair was the same kinky black as Robert's, and he had Robert's coal black eyes, but slightly lighter skin. As did Cassie, although a lighter version still, since her biological mother was white. "Oh my!" was all I could get out.

"Heh, heh, I should have told you sooner, but the occasion never seemed to present itself, so Jose and I decided to tell you this way, when he didn't have his tour guide duty. His mother, Cecilia, and I were a couple for many years after I arrived here at the Monarch Sanctuary. She just couldn't bring herself to live permanently on top of the mountain, so I would stay here in town with her as much as I could. We loved one another very much, and wanted to marry, but the living arrangements were difficult. Cecilia needed to be close to her parents here in town. We just maintained our relationship in either her place or mine. Then Jose came along. He needed to live in the village to attend school." Robert glanced fondly over at Jose. "Sadly, Cecilia passed away eight years ago." His eyes watered at that, and he brushed with his napkin to quickly dispel the moisture.

Jose, too, sniffed a bit, the emotion still raw even after all the years. "Mom always dreamed that I would one day take Dad's place in research one day. I plan to attend university this fall to get started on my study of entomology. I hope to make her memory proud and do well for Dad, too."

All the while, I sat entranced—speechless. What could I say to all this? It was so shocking, so sudden. I kept turning from Robert to Jose, wondering what to say. Finally, I thought of a question. "So, Jose, when you met Cassie the first time by taking a tour group up with her, did you ever suspect she might be your half-sister?"

Jose chuckled nervously, taking a sip of his mineral water. "Uh, no, not at all—I really had no idea. Dad mentioned to me after she was here, that he once had a relationship with a woman in the States, but nothing like that. Until, that is," he paused, looking over at Robert, "until a few years back when he traveled to the U.S. Then he told me all about Cassie. I hope one day that we can have a nice brother-sister relationship. I would love that," he looked up and smiled. "I don't have any other siblings, you know."

"There is so much here to put together. Wow! We need to figure out how to help that happen. The present time is difficult, what with the lockdowns in the cities, but Cassie is still here in Mexico—in Puebla—waiting to go back home."

"Right. Dad explained some of that to me the other day. We are so isolated up here that it sounds so unreal. Everything in lockdown—wow!"

It was then that I noticed Jose's accent. Even though he spoke English fluently, he carried with it the Spanish accent. No doubt Spanish was his first language, but Robert saw to it that he became bilingual from the start. "So, Jose, tell me more about yourself. I want to know everything! This is so unbelievable but exciting, too. Do you realize that Cassie is my adopted daughter and now I hear that you are her half-brother? A lot for me to absorb, here. I was thinking that Robert was going to show me some new butterfly species or something. Not his son!" I chuckled, taking a sip off my mineral water.

Jose toyed with his glass of soda, seeming to concentrate on how much ice was in the glass. He also took a sip before speaking. "Well, what more is there? I grew up here in Angangueo, attending the small school here, and graduated high school five years ago. I have been working as a tour guide to the Monarch Sanctuary ever since, helping Dad out when I can, and learning what I can from him in my spare time. I've been saving up for the university and am looking forward to going this fall." He finished simply, hoping that was enough to answer my question.

"Okay. I guess that's good for now. Hope we can share more as time goes on. I don't know how long I'll be here at the Sanctuary."

At that point, Jose fixed his gaze from me to Robert, taking in the fact that we must indeed be a couple by now. It felt a bit strange, since he still missed his mom, Cecilia. "Sure, sure. We'll talk more." Nervously, Jose set his glass down, and wiped his mouth with a napkin.

It was Robert who broke the awkward silence. "So, Tully, what do you hear from Cassie? Any news yet as to when they can get back home?"

"Nothing yet. Not for certain. So, she just waits and hopes."

"I would love to meet with her again before she leaves—you know, talk about the fact that we are related," Jose added quickly.

"Yes—that would be really nice. Let's see how everything goes." I peered over to Robert for support.

"For sure. We'll be in touch, of course." Robert took my hand and patted it.

The three of us finished our lunch and then Jose headed back to the stable. Robert took me shopping while in town, slowly ambling back to the hotel for the night. We would ride back up the mountain first thing in the morning with Jose's new tour group.

Chapter 27

Cassie

"What? What is it you are saying?" I took a breath, holding the phone away from my face for a moment.

"Yes. I'm saying that I finally found out that Jose is your half-brother. Robert invited me down the mountain to show me a surprise. Jose was the surprise." Tully took a sip off her coffee, allowing me to process for a moment.

"Are you kidding me? I had no idea when I met Jose during the horse ride up the mountain—either time that I went. No way!"

It was the day after Tully's surprise luncheon with Jose, and she called before setting off back up to the mountain top. There was no Wi-Fi reception up there.

"Right. Well, you both have the same father but different mothers. That accounts for your difference in appearance, for one thing. His mother was Latina, and yours, white. But you can sort of see it in your tight frizzy hair. Both of you have that from your father, right?"

"Well, yes. I get that much. Okay. So where is his mom?"

"She passed away eight years ago, sadly. Cancer, I believe. So here we are. Robert and I are officially dating, I guess you could say." Tully laughed nervously, taking another swallow of her coffee.

"I suppose I should try to get back up there and have a brother-sister chat, right? Before I get my ticket to fly home to the States to see Abbie."

"That would be a good idea, I think. See what you can do to get up here. I know it's hard to travel right now, what with the lockdowns."

"Okay, Mom. Wait until I tell Luis! He won't believe it—crazy development. I have a Latino brother!" I chuckled as I said this. "I'll get word to you when I'm coming."

By the time I got off the phone with Tully, I received another call. This time it was the U.S. Consulate. They had managed to obtain a ticket to L.A. and on to Seattle for me. But only one. Luis had to stay for the time being, and I would leave in a few days. Elated, I called Luis, who happened to be volunteering at the hospital for the day. "Luis, guess what? I leave for the U.S. in four days! I'll be with our Abbie soon. Sorry, there is only one ticket. Will you be okay with this?"

"Sure, sure. I'll get a ticket soon, I'm certain. Go ahead and get with our little girl. She needs you. I'll be home soon, and we can talk more. Gotta go for now."

Chapter 28

CASSIE

"The rain begins with a single drop."
—Manal al-Sharif

There was to be no brother-sister get together. I was on my way to the States in four days, and never looked back. I could hardly wait to see Abbie and my sis, Jasmine. As the plane sped its way northward in the sky, I leaned back, sipping on a glass of Chardonay to calm my nerves. I finally got it—a ticket home. A ticket to be with my only child, Abbie. When I left my little girl, I was planning to only be away for two weeks, not two months. What changes would I see in my little one that I had missed out on? Abbie was four years old, and at that age, each day could bring something new. I had missed out. A tear slid down my cheek, and I brushed it away with my napkin. I vowed to myself to never leave Abbie again, at least not until she reached eighteen. There was so much to make up for. As I contemplated this, I made mental notes of just what Abbie and I would do together once reunited. Then I realized that the country was in the middle of a pandemic, so some things would have to wait. *At least, we will finally be together.* After finishing my wine, I slipped my mask back on, as it was a requirement on board the plane. I closed my eyes, imagining the rains of the Northwest, and smiled. Soon I would be there. Abbie and I could walk in the rain together, lifting our faces into the falling droplets.

PART 3

The Northwest:

Oregon/Washington

Chapter 29

CASSIE

"Soul mate and rain are a perfect combination."
—Amrapali Gupta

"What are you telling me?" I asked on the phone, as Luis and I talked to one another for the first time since I had arrived at Jasmine's house in Springville three days ago. The phone lines were still intermittent.

"I'm saying that the hospital here has offered me a job. They are extremely short-handed for doctors because of the pandemic. So many patients keep pouring in."

My breathing stopped—I felt in shock. "But we live here. You have your medical practice here. I need you here. So does Abbie. What are you thinking? You can't live down there indefinitely." I struggled to maintain my composure, but inwardly panicked. *This can't be. Things were going from bad to worse.*

"Cassie, I am desperately needed here. This is a crisis of global proportions. Surely you see that, Sweetheart," Luis added, hoping to appeal to her better nature.

"No! I won't have it! You can't stay in Mexico! Come on, Luis. We are a family now." I felt tears forming behind my eyes.

"It's just until the pandemic ends. That can't be for long. I'm sure of it. Besides," he said, sensing my breakdown into tears, "I can't get a ticket home yet anyway."

"But you need to keep trying at the consulate until you get one. Please!" I tensed, my insides churning, turning into a clutching pain in my gut.

Luis sighed. "This is bigger than our own situation. I am a physician. I took an oath to help others. You have to try to understand! These are my people—I grew up here, remember? Just bear with me. You are up there with Abbie now, and Jasmine's family. You can do your work remotely and keep up with that as well." I sniffed and was silent; he continued. "Soon, Tully will get a ticket back, and perhaps our friends as well. Please be patient. This is unprecedented. We haven't had a global pandemic in a hundred years. Cassie?" He stopped, sensing that I was refusing to speak.

"I don't' like this. Not one bit. Abbie and I need you. Plus, at the hospital there, you are exposed to the virus every day."

"I know. But Puebla and my family also need me. And you have your grandmother to check in on, too. Okay? I love you."

"No not okay. But at least, I am here. I love finally being with Abbie. Soon we will walk together in the fall rains again."

"That's my girl. Give Abbie a hug and kiss from me."

I hung up, flinging myself onto the bed for a good cry. Soon, Abbie heard me crying and entered the room. "Mommie, what's wrong?" Abbie jumped onto the bed and petted my messy hair.

"I'm fine, really. I just miss your daddy. He'll be home soon, don't worry," I added quickly, sensing Abbie's reaction. "Let's watch on the news when we can expect some rain. We can go outside in it like we love to do, alright?" I tried to brighten up, blowing my nose as I stood up, smoothing down my hair. It was hopeless, really—my hair, that is.

"Sure, Mommie. I like that!" Abbie took my hand and led the way to the living room, where we sat down together to check the weather forecast. It was time to seize the moment—I was again with Abbie, and that's what mattered most right now.

As we watched the weather forecast, I thought back to the day I had arrived here three days prior. Jasmine had pulled up to her house after picking me up at the Seattle airport, and my heart had lurched, barely containing myself in my eagerness to scoop up Abbie in my arms. As Jasmine unlocked the door, she commented, "Well, I don't know how the house will look by now. John is here with the kids, you know." She chuckled, glancing over my way, but I was already stepping inside and casting my gaze around, looking for Abbie. I heard child voices, following their laughing and shouting in the living room.

"Abbie—Josh—Josie—I'm here! What's going on?" I saw that the couch cushions had been removed and the sofa made into a fort with a blanket. No children were visible as yet.

"We're in a fort! Come find us!" a child's voice chortled.

"Okay, here I come!" I lifted the blanket to find the three children huddled underneath. A few toys were scattered inside.

"Hi Aunt Cassie. Do you like our fort?" Josh was the one who greeted me. NotAbbie. It was as if I had only been away for ten minutes instead of two months. Abbie was silent, just staring at me somberly.

"Abbie come give me a hug," I begged, disappointed at the cool reception. I stepped back, waiting for the three to come out from under the blanket. No one came out. They continued their pretend playtime, heedless to my entreaties. When they finally did at lunchtime, Abbie greeted me with a shy smile, running to sit at the table with her cousins for grilled cheese sandwiches.

Winter

The sky spits snow, miniscule icy granules.

*Frost clings to rooftops and grass, white as
the hair on an old woman.*

*Trees stand, naked and swarthy, a stark reminder
of old age and death to follow.*

*Winds rattle the trees' arms- shivering from the
blasts—but they are spared no mercy.*

*Relentless, the gales continue, as humans also
bend in submission, holding onto hats.*

*At long last, spring rains deliver the land
from freezing temperatures.*

*A welcome balm, coaxing the trees
to bud once more.*

Linda L. Graham

Chapter 30

CASSIE

"A wind has blown the rain away and blown the sky away and all the leaves away, and the trees stand still. I think, I too, have known autumn too long."

—E.E. Cummings

Abbie and I held hands, strolling in the rain. In the distance, ocean waves could be heard, as we had finally arrived at our beach home in Lincoln City two days before. "Mommie, when is Daddy coming home? I miss him."

I looked down at my little girl, giving her hand a gentle squeeze. "I miss him, too, little one. I really don't know. There are many sick people where he is, and he is trying to help them."

"Okay. Well, my heart feels sick, too. I really want to see him."

"I know. Me too. But we have one another here, and Daddy would want us to stay happy. Plus, look up! It's raining now!" We turned our faces upward, tongues sticking out to taste the droplets, tepid and slightly salty. The trees framed the rain, allowing an open space in the overhead sky for the rain to fall. We giggled together, enjoying the moment—the moment I had longed for all those days and weeks in Mexico. There, I was without Abbie and without the cleansing moisture and fir trees of home. I savored the feeling, wishing it to last a lifetime. "Say, how about we go to the ice cream shop and get a cone?"

"Yes! I bet I can beat you there!" Abbie took off.

"Wait for me at the corner, Abbie," I called after her, quickening my step just in case. After the initial cool greeting at Jasmine's when I first arrived back, Abbie warmed up to me after about two days. I had lost those two months without her, and it was a bit longer than I had originally imagined to be reunited with my little girl. We had to make the best of it now.

THE NEXT DAY, WHEN THE PHONE RANG, I SAW A PHONE NUMBER I didn't recognize, originating from Mexico. "Hello?" I said, tensing, and sitting down at the kitchen table.

"Cass? Just me, Luis. Sorry to startle you with the unknown number. The hospital allowed me to try to call from their line. I can't seem to get a call through on my cell." Luis hesitated, allowing me to process that it was Luis calling.

"Are you okay?" Fear that he was sick gripped my heart.

"Yes. Sure. I'm strong. Plus, I'm taking precautions, wearing a mask, washing my hands, wearing gloves and my surgical clothes. I shower here before leaving. No worry." He chuckled nervously.

"So, did you call to let me know you are coming home? Abbie and I need you."

"Uh, actually, I called to say that the rest are leaving for home in just three days. The consulate got them all tickets."

"So, Tully, Claire, Preston, and Tommy?"

"For now, Tommy is remaining here to be with Viviana. Their baby is due in just three months. He wants to be here for that."

My mind was racing. *Why hadn't he mentioned that he was returning?* "And you? When are you returning?" Stubbornly, I awaited his response. It was slow in coming.

Luis drew a deep breath before speaking. "Cass," his voice took on an impatient tone. "We discussed this already. I can't leave right now. My family here needs me, and the hospital needs me. There are many people there, all suffering through this pandemic."

"Luis, were you offered a ticket home? I want to know. Tell me," I demanded. I heard my voice, which had risen sharply.

"Well, yes, Sweetie they did. But I had to refuse it. The ticket will go to someone else who needs to get back. Sorry," he finished slowly, certain of the explosive reply.

"What? I can't believe it! You don't care about me or Abbie, who told me that her heart is sick. She needs you, Luis. So do I." By now I was shouting.

"But Cassie, just try to understand what I'm trying to do here. Please."

"You just don't get it! If you can't understand how much we need you here, then don't bother to come back!" At that, the anger and hurt rose in me, and I slammed down my phone, disconnecting the call that was always so difficult to connect. I had no idea how or when to tell him my latest development. *How will I tell him I'm pregnant? This is more than I can handle right now.* I slumped in my chair and sobbed.

Chapter 31

Cassie

Abbie and I settled into a mundane routine, now at home in Lincoln City. Oregon was on lockdown, so our outings outside of the house were limited. We took daily strolls along the beach, and if the weather permitted, Abbie brought her sand bucket and shovel, and we created crude sandcastles. The following day, we went back to see that the incoming tide had washed our sandcastle away during the night. Some days, we walked in a nearby park, nestled in among the tall firs. The branches swayed in the wind, a desolate, lonesome song. During those walks, we lifted our faces to the mists, relishing the cleansing moisture. All the while, Abbie and I missed Luis, but he wasn't coming home anytime soon.

During the rare times Luis and I spoke on the phone, our conversation was terse—stilted. We no longer had much to say to one another. He knew that Abbie and I missed him and hoped for him to return. I realized that he was there in Puebla to stay, at least, for as long as the pandemic was spiraling out of control. "So how is Abbie?" Luis attempted to bring up a safe topic on one such call.

"Well, you know. She loves to go to the beach when the weather is mild, but we can't go many places due to the lockdown. But we're managing," I finished nervously.

"Good, good. Give her a hug and kiss from me."

"Okay, sure. She's in bed right now or I would have her come to the phone."

"Next time. Gotta go." And with that, our strained dialog came to a swift end. I heard the connection click off abruptly, and I held my phone, staring into it for a second.

How will I ever break the news to him that we have a baby on the way? My breath caught, feeling as though Abbie and I had been abandoned forever. I lay down on the sofa and cried myself to sleep. It was as if a dark cloud had settled over our home. Indeed, the pandemic was having its ominous effect.

THE NEXT DAY, CLAIRE CALLED. "WE'RE HOME! WE JUST GOT IN late last night into Frisco." The joy and relief were evident in her voice. I felt a bit envious at her obvious happiness.

"Great! How was the flight?" I hung onto the phone, wondering how much longer I would have to wait for Luis to finally make his way back home. *You'd think he was already home, for all he seems to care,* I was thinking. *Actually, he was,* I thought with a start. Puebla is his childhood home.

"Well, everyone is masked, and they don't serve any beverages. Just the flight. But we're so thankful to be back," Claire finished.

"Yeah, I can imagine. I was too. Did you see Luis much?"

"No, not really. He keeps to himself and is working at the hospital constantly. Plus, I heard that he sleeps and stays at the hospital to try to prevent his family from getting the virus." Claire paused, not sure of what else Cassie would ask.

"Right. So, did he get a ticket to return when the rest of you did?" I dreaded the answer, although Luis had already admitted as much.

"Yes, well, Tully returned to L.A. with us, and then she took the flight out to Seattle from there, and Preston and I got ours to San Francisco. We only had three days' notice that our tickets were issued, and we had to be all set to leave right away. I guess Luis gave his ticket to a stranger needing to get back to the States."

At that, I choked, swallowing hard. "That's what Luis said. It's hard for me to accept that. We waited all those weeks to get out of Mexico to be with Abbie, and then he refused to go." The bitterness crept into my voice, but I couldn't help it.

"Cass, are you okay? Luis is doing a good thing, you know. He is a doctor, and they desperately need him there."

"I know that. But Abbie and I need him, too. You have no idea."

"I think I do know. This pandemic is difficult, at best." Claire attempted to be supportive, but it wasn't working.

"Claire, I will tell you something if you can keep it a secret for now." I hesitated, waiting for her to say something.

"Of course. We're besties, right girlfriend?"

"Uh, Claire, I'm having another baby—I'm pregnant. And I haven't told Luis, at least not yet. I just can't bring myself to say it when he calls. We aren't on the best of terms right now." I stopped, reaching for a tissue and blew my nose.

"Oh, Cassie! You need to tell him—as soon as possible. And, by the way, congratulations! You are blessed with another one on the way. Do you know if it is a girl or boy yet?"

"Well, I found out just yesterday. A girl. I want to name her Amalia if Luis agrees."

"You two need to talk things out. Give him a call, if you can get through, that is."

"I don't know. It just doesn't seem right to tell him over the phone like that, especially when he doesn't want to come home." I sniffed and reached for another tissue.

"Think about it. He would want to know."

"I don't want the baby to be the reason he comes back. Later, he may resent the baby." At that moment, another call was attempting to come through. "Gotta go, Claire. I'll call you again later. I have an incoming."

It was Tully. "Cassie, I'm home! It feels so good to be back."

I took a deep breath. "Great, Mom. Glad you made it back safely. How was your flight?" I tried to distract her and myself from any topic pertaining to Luis, but eventually, she brought it up.

"Luis is working all the time at the hospital—even living there. Does he call you often?"

There it was. The tension between Luis and me. I avoided her by saying, "Mom, Abbie is waking up. I need to get her some breakfast. Let's talk later, okay?"

Chapter 32

CASSIE

Eventually, Abbie and I drove up to Springville to greet Tully and visit Jasmine and her family. Since I had to work remotely, it was easy enough to bring my work with me on my laptop. Currently, I was writing a feature on places to walk outdoors while visiting Lincoln City. Abbie and I had already trolled many of those places together.

"Cassie, wait up!" It was Jasmine, who had just arrived as well. She ran to catch up with us, and we entered Tully's condo together. She gave me a quick hug, and Abbie jumped into her arms. "I've missed you, little one," Jasmine declared. Abbie emitted a squeal of happiness, and the three of us went inside where Tully awaited to pass out hugs for each of us.

"Aunt Jasmine, where's Josh and Josie?" Abbie looked up expectantly.

"Well, they're in online school today. You can play with them later."

"It's so good to see you here in my home instead of in Puebla, Cassie." Tully seemed genuinely happy to be back, as was I, although I had mixed feelings since Luis remained in Mexico.

"You too, Mom." I smiled wanly, hoping she didn't notice my true apprehensions. I was even having a bit of morning nausea with the pregnancy. *Did it show?* I wondered. It wasn't quite noon, but I still felt nauseous. "Uh, Mom, do you have any Seven Up? I need a little if you do."

Suddenly, Tully's radar shifted. "Why? Are you sick? Is it possibly the virus? Any other symptoms?"

"No, just a bit of upset stomach." I shrugged, hoping she wouldn't persist.

"You three come into the kitchen. I'll get us all something to drink, and later fix some lunch." Jasmine and I followed Mom into the kitchen, but Abbie went into the spare bedroom where a box of toys was kept for Tully's grandchildren.

Tully served lunch shortly after the beverages, consisting of turkey sandwiches and vegetable soup. I decided the fare seemed bland enough for my queasy stomach, but as I ate, my stomach thought otherwise. "Excuse me," I blurted before lurching to the bathroom and heaving up all my lunch thus far. I waited in the bathroom a bit, hoping my stomach would settle down enough to return to the table, but it wasn't having it. Dry heaves took over. When I was certain it was over, I slowly stumbled back into the kitchen. Tully focused on me like a laser, as if dissecting my insides, attempting to figure out what was wrong. Embarrassed, I sat down, pushing my plate and bowl to the side. "I think I'll stick with the Seven Up if you don't mind."

Even Jasmine gave me the once over. "What is it, Sis? You okay?"

"Yes, what's going on, Sweetie," Tully chimed in.

"Oh, just a touchy stomach from the drive up, I imagine. Really, I'm okay." My eyes must have belied my statement. I chuckled nervously.

"I don't think that's it. You are either coming down with Covid or something, or you're pregnant. Which is it?" Tully persisted; her eyes boring into mine.

"How do I know? I'm not a doctor."

"Well, you might know if there's a chance you are pregnant," Tully insisted. Jasmine nodded in agreement.

"Alright you two, I'm pregnant. Are you satisfied?" I retorted, refusing to look up, and focused on my glass of soda.

Tully clapped her hands in glee. "Yes! I knew it! I can hardly wait! Another grandchild! Do you know if a girl or boy yet?"

"Yes, a girl. I hope to name her Amalia. But Luis doesn't know yet, and you mustn't tell him. I will eventually."

"Yay! We know first! Gottta love that, right Mom?" Jasmine glanced over to Tully, both smiling from ear to ear. "But why haven't you told Luis yet?"

"Well, uh, he and I aren't exactly getting along over the phone. I think he should come home, but he feels he needs to stay and help out in Mexico. Abbie and I need him here. He needs to be with us. Then I'll tell him." As I admitted this, I felt a bit foolish. I looked up at my mom and sister sheepishly.

"Well, dear, that may be some time from now. You must tell him soon." Tully took my hand in hers, but in doing so, seemed to emphasize the advice.

"I agree with Mom. What if, God forbid, something was to go wrong with you or the baby? That would be a horrible way for him to find out, right?"

I sighed before answering. "You're both right. I'll let him know soon. Don't worry. I just need him to focus on me when we talk, not on a patient in the next room."

Chapter 33

CASSIE

MAY 2020

The days crawled by, with Luis working in the hospital in Mexico, and me, here in Oregon, enduring morning sickness while caring for Abbie. Luis didn't call for the next few days, so I didn't tell him about the baby-to-be yet. When I visited my gynecologist last week, a due date was set for early January of 2021. Where would Luis be at that time? How would I cope until then? For that matter, how would little Abbie cope? Each weekday, after breakfast with Abbie, I sat down at my laptop to attempt to work from home. My feature stories sounded bland and mundane, even to me. How would they be embraced in the local newspaper?

Finally, I received a call. "Cassie, hey. I know you are trying to write from home, as we all are, but I need you to try to spice your stories up a bit. They're sounding dull, you know?" It was Sharon, my editor.

"Uh, sure. Any suggestions?"

"Actually, I do have a few. I have a couple of leads on interviews you can do by phone. One is for a retired police chief. You in?"

"Sure, sure. Just give me the contact info. I'll get on it right away." I scribbled down the phone number and name, and dutifully made the call. My heart just wasn't in it anymore. Everything seemed like such a chore, and I didn't feel well. Plus, the whole Luis-is-away thing. I tried to liven up my writing with better adjectives and action words. Maybe that will help, I reasoned. While I wrote, Abbie had learned to use her time with watercolors or crayons, sitting next to me at the kitchen table. We could get through this, I told myself. In the back of my mind, however, I pictured Luis, masked and gloved, tending to countless sick people, some dying of the dreaded Covid virus. *How long would he keep going? Did he even miss us like we did him?*

As I sat at my laptop, the words to the page wouldn't come. I glanced over to Abbie, who was busily coloring in her coloring book full of pictures of various types of butterflies. She looked up then. "Mommy, look! I made this butterfly a blue one. Do you like it?"

"Yes, very original," I replied, chuckling to myself. It was the outline of a Monarch, but in Abbie's world, it could be any color. Since I couldn't come up with anything original to say in my feature story, I decided to call Claire. She was always good therapy for me—a true friend.

Claire picked up after the first ring. "Hey, girlfriend. How are you feeling?"

"Oh, still have the morning nausea. What's going on there? Do you or Preston hear from Tommy at all?"

"Well, in fact, he called Preston yesterday. Viviana is doing well and expecting the baby in the last week of October or so. Tommy's working for Esteban at the Puebla City Hall."

"Good, good," I answered absently. "And you?"

"Well, you know, lock down and all that. I'm doing some work online here at home. I sure hope they lift the lockdown soon. So have you told Luis about your baby yet?"

"Uh, no. He hasn't called in a while. I still don't know how to broach the topic, with his rushed attitude, calling from the hospital. I—I just don't know what to do, Claire." I sniffed and grabbed a tissue.

"Well, if you're asking me, I would say to just call him, and leave a message that you need to talk to him about something important, and that you need some private time. That should get his attention, don't you think?" Claire tittered, waiting for my answer.

I hesitated, then, "Yeah, I guess you're right. I'll try that soon. When I have time to myself without Abbie listening or interrupting. I'll have to figure out when. Maybe when she's napping."

"Good. No matter what, you need to tell him, and soon. It will be okay. He's your husband, remember?"

"You're right. You are such a good friend, Claire. Thanks for the advice. Gotta run. Abbie needs lunch."

"Til next time. Call me anytime."

We clicked off, and I sat, mesmerized by Abbie's doodling, as she chattered to me happily about her artwork. Then I made grilled cheese sandwiches for her and myself, feeling alone and abandoned, wondering when to make the call to Luis.

Chapter 34

LUIS

The workday at the hospital here in Puebla seemed endless. I started by five in the morning, and didn't stop, even to eat, until at least five in the evening—sometimes later. I grabbed a little dinner in the hospital cafeteria before collapsing onto a spare bed set up for me in the hospital. Early the next morning, I began once again. The days flew by, with barely a moment for me to think about Cassie or Abbie, so far away from here. The sickness and suffering gripped my whole being—I just couldn't' abandon these people. At least, by sleeping and living in the hospital, I didn't run the risk of infecting my family here in Puebla.

To say that I missed Cassie and Abbie was an understatement. Underneath all the desperation in the hospital, I hoped that they were doing fine without me. At least, Cassie had her family not too far away. That would have to be enough until this horrible affliction subsided. I didn't even dream of them anymore; I was just too exhausted at night, and went into an exhausted stupor, my body attempting to recover from the day.

"Luis, call home." It was my father leaving a message on my phone. I hadn't looked at messages in several days. Before I began my rounds, I called him back.

"Hey, Dad what's going on?"

"Uh, Luis. Good you returned my call. Yeah, I think you need to get in touch with Cassie. She called here last night, hoping to speak with you when you aren't busy."

"Oh, wow," I chuckled. "I don't know when that will happen; I'm busy from the moment I get up in the morning until falling asleep at night. It's crazy here."

"Well, she sounded like it was important. Try to make some time today, for her sake. Okay?"

I took a deep breath. "Okay, Dad. I'll see what I can do. Everyone healthy there?"

"So far, we're doing alright. Well, I won't keep you. Take care of yourself, Son."

"Sure, Dad. Thanks for the call and good to hear from you." I sat on the edge of my bed, trying to think of what Cassie might want. It was unusual for her to call my family instead of me. What could she want? I'd have to see when I had time to call. I was due in for my rounds in five minutes, so it would have to wait for now.

The day flew by in a blur, and I didn't get around to calling Cassie. It just wasn't possible. To be perfectly honest, I dismissed the idea from my mind the moment I saw my first patient. I encountered a continuous succession of sick and dying patients. Who had time to consider personal life? Once more, I fell into the makeshift bed set up for me, and immediately elapsed into a deep sleep, only to be awakened the next morning by my alarm at four thirty. I had just enough time to take a shower and stumble to the elevator to start my rounds.

Three days after Dad called, it occurred to me that he had asked me to call Cassie. Why did I forget that? I felt a twinge of guilt, but at the moment, I was on my way to visit yet another Covid patient recently admitted to the I.C.U. ward. There was no way I could pause to make a phone call. Soon after seeing this patient, I moved on to another, and totally put the call out of my mind. I was inundated with sickness and dying. That night, before I crawled into bed, I noticed a phone message from Cassie. I didn't even have the energy to listen to it. *I'll check later*, I told myself, and turned off the light.

Chapter 35

CASSIE

No return phone call, I thought to myself as I got out the cereal to feed Abbie her breakfast. What shall I do? I've tried to contact Luis, but he doesn't return my calls. I even tried contacting him through Esteban. I thought that would help but so far, nothing. Guess I'll try calling Claire to see what she thinks I should do now.

"Hey, Girlfriend. About time you called me back. How are you?"

"Oh, Claire, I don't know what to do. Luis hasn't returned my calls. I guess he's working all the time. No time for me or Abbie."

"Yeah, that's hard, I can imagine. But just think what all he is struggling with in Mexico. That has to be mind-numbing and physically draining. You can't force him to call, I suppose. Plus, your news is not easy to tell him from up here. Just give it time."

"Maybe he doesn't care about us anymore. It's all about 'my people'. I'm sick to death of hearing about it."

"Oh, Cassie. That can't be true. He is just doing what he committed himself to when he became a doctor, right?"

"I guess. How are you guys doing? Staying well I hope?"

"Yes. Both Preston and I are working remotely from home. Hope it gets better out there soon."

We said our goodbyes, and I turned my attention to Abbie, all the while pondering what to do about talking to Luis, and my impending news of a baby on the way.

I WAS JOLTED OUT OF A FITFUL SLEEP THE FOLLOWING NIGHT around one a.m. "Cass, it's Luis. Dad told me you were trying to get hold of me. Is everything okay up there?" The sound of his familiar voice roused me out of my slumber. Instantly, I felt the old resentment creeping in.

"Well, well, well, you finally called. Why now? Aren't you busy with a sick patient?" I regretted the question as soon as it left my lips. *Why did I react like that?*

"Well, yes, as a matter of fact, I am overwhelmed with ailing patients, all fighting for their lives. What do you want that is more urgent than that?" Luis snapped back, also regretting his reaction. He couldn't help himself. He was exhausted beyond tiredness, producing an emotional abyss he felt himself falling into. How was he to expect her to understand what he was going through?

"I guess nothing. Nothing is more urgent than that. Thanks for calling, even though it's the middle of the night. No time for us other than that, I suppose." I clicked the phone off and settled back onto my pillow. I sighed, trying to settle down once more. Sleep eluded me for the rest of the night. I awakened to Abbie's insistence for breakfast, bouncing on the bed until I dragged myself up. I planted my feet on the floor and willed myself to stagger into the kitchen for cold cereal. I hated myself for hanging up on Luis, but how could I share our news with both of us resenting one another? What was I to do?

Chapter 36

TULLY

TWO WEEKS PRIOR, SEPTEMBER 2020, IN THE BUTTERFLY SANCTUARY, MICHOACAN

The day was cold; a biting wind penetrated our jackets, and the horses snorted in protest at the heavy wind tossing their manes and tails. It was already early fall; leaves were changing their colors from green to yellow and red. Jose brought up the two horses we usually rode, and the tour group Jose had led for the day returned with us. I was told only this morning that Robert had arranged for us to descend the mountain top for a dinner date. All the group was silent, concentrating their holds on the reins, hoping that the horses would remain steady and not bolt from a falling tree branch. I stared straight ahead, my thoughts wandering. *Why come down today? The cabin feels warm and cozy, and we have plenty of provisions for now.* Robert had insisted it was important, so I reluctantly agreed. It was true that we did get cabin fever at times.

At one point, a tourist's mount stumbled, snorting loudly, and then regained its balance. Jose jerked the reins on his lead horse to glance back, making sure everyone was okay. He grinned, turned, and prodded his steed onward. By the time we reached the village of Angangueo, my teeth were chattering from the cold. *How many more years could Robert possibly live up here?* I wondered. I know I'm reaching my limit, as far as age, to be gallivanting up and down a mountainside in Mexico on horseback. It seemed like a young person's folly.

At last, we reached the village, and Jose led our horses to the stable, although I doubted the horses needed any guidance. They were always anxious to get back to their stalls where hay and oats awaited them. As we entered, the wind whipped around the rough boards of the rustic building, tearing into the cozy stalls, lined in straw. The musty smell of horse and hay was comforting; I couldn't blame the horses for yearning to return to their dwelling. Sometimes Robert lingered with Jose in the stable, chatting and assisting him with brushing down the steeds. Today, I even helped a little, brushing down my mount named Destiny. I enjoyed riding him; he was old and reliable, but also a former beauty in a dapple gray. I spoke softly to him as I brushed, thanking him for carrying me safely down the mountainside. It seemed that work horses such as these were not appreciated enough. Their lives consisted of the mundane plodding up and down, carrying people who weren't always kind to them or knowledgeable on how to ride. The horses' mouths were often raw and sore from the bit when amateur riders pulled too hard on the reins, or they were humiliated when their sides were prodded mercilessly with the riders' boots. They bore these indignities and cruelties with stoicism. I wished I could demonstrate to each horse how much I cared for them. At the least, I could help Destiny a little. When I finished brushing him, I offered him a small apple I had tucked into my pocket, and he munched it appreciatively.

After thirty minutes or so in the stable, Robert and I said our goodbyes to Jose and ambled down the street to the hotel eatery. I still wondered why we had journeyed to town this day, but said nothing, smiling up at Robert and enjoying the views in the scenic little town. Small businesses lined the street, most located in buildings which appeared to date back to colonial days and partially obscured in ivy-covered stucco. Red-topped roofs dotted the village, all cheerily reminding me of better days to come. "Robert, why are we here today? I can't stand the suspense!"

"Oh, you'll see very soon. Just wait a bit more." He smiled mysteriously, taking my hand, and swinging our arms as we sauntered down the street. We ascended the steps to the historic hotel and wandered down the hall to the open dining room. A waiter evidently knew we were coming and led the way to a table covered in a white tablecloth, already set for two, and pulled out a chair for me to sit. I obliged, and glanced again at Robert, who appeared nonchalant, his face a blank, as he nodded to the waiter, saying, "Gracias, Jeraldo." Immediately, Jeraldo brought out a bottle of champagne and two fluted glasses. He poured some into each glass, silently nodded to Robert, and left. I sat in bewilderment, wondering what awaited next. "Okay, what is going on? Are you telling me yet?" I giggled.

"First, I would like to say 'salute' to our relationship and time together. May there be many more." With that, Robert clinked his glass to mine, and we took a sip together. We set our glasses down, and he took my hand in his. "Tully, I'm not very good at this. I don't know how to say it—but I—I want to ask if you will marry me. I love you and want to spend the rest of my life with you."

I gasped a little and stared into his eyes. "I love you too, Robert. Very much, I'm realizing. However, would getting married mean that we live here up on the mountain in the cabin, and have to ride horses every time we want to come to town? We aren't getting any younger, you know." I was half teasing him, but also really wanted to know what he was thinking.

"No, of course not," he grinned. I have been training Jose to take my place, and he will also attend the university soon to complete his studies in entomology. I need to retire—I just have to finalize arranging all of that with Jose."

"Oh! I guess you've thought of everything. So, where then?" I persisted, always the realist. "I mean, I love you, but we have to think practically, don't we?"

"Is that a yes?" Robert asked, taking my hand again, and looking intently into my eyes over a sip of champagne.

"Well, uh, yes, yes! Could we live where I live now, in Springville, perhaps?"

"Sure. Anywhere but this mountaintop, I suppose. Plus, Springville would put me near Cassie and my little granddaughter. Our granddaughter." Robert leaned across the table, kissing me on the lips. We laughed, drank more champagne until I felt heady from it all, and then ordered our meal. The waiter already knew what Robert had preordered, and magically, the first course was brought out—a fresh green salad and a cup of tortilla soup. More champagne followed, then the main course—whole baked tilapia with potatoes and peas in a cream sauce. Dessert consisted of Mexican "milk" cake, served with a strawberry compote. I felt stuffed but content.

"So, Tully, is it alright with you if we stay over here for the night and ride up again in the morning?" Robert picked up the check and handed Geraldo his card.

"Well, I didn't plan on this and didn't bring my overnight bag," I said, disappointed that I would spoil the moment.

"I anticipated that and took the liberty of bringing a few of your "essentials" in my backpack. I think you'll find enough in there to get by for one night," he chuckled.

"Oh, well, in that case, okay. I hope you brought all of my necessaries. But I need to take another walk before we go to our room.

I am too full." So, it was settled. We took a long walk, leisurely strolling down the main street, and stopped in a few shops to pick up a few more snacks and basics for the evening. As we shopped, Robert remembered that he had neglected to bring my toothbrush. So, I picked one out—a green one. And we were getting married soon! The thought was exhilarating! No date or details, but it was a start. We could talk more in the morning.

Entering our room of the hotel, we heard the wind pick up. The room felt cold and uninviting. We set down our few possessions and snacks and huddled close together under the thick layer of blankets on the bed. As the wind howled, the ancient windowpanes shuddered. Dry leaves slashed against the glass, pinging out a forlorn song. I snuggled closer to Robert, my head nestled in the nook of Robert's shoulder. I inhaled the scent of his aftershave, savoring the fragrance—his scent. Life was good, at least for the moment—the dreaded pandemic relegated to a distant place far away. The world could wait. We had our own little hideaway up here in a remote village atop a mountain in Mexico.

Chapter 37

LUIS

OCTOBER 2020

I kept up my nearly constant vigil in the Puebla hospital, caring for the sick and dying brought into the overcrowded hospital. As I passed through the lobby at three in the morning, having just tended to yet another person suffering in the I.C.U., I nearly ran into my sister, Viviana. Tommy had dropped her off at the entrance, since visitors were not allowed, but she was admitted into the hospital because she was well into labor. A nurse had seated her in a wheelchair, and Viviana happened to look up as another contraction passed. "Luis is that really you?" she gasped in jagged breaths, seeing only my bloodshot eyes above my mask. She must have noticed the tired drooping of my shoulders.

"Viv, what are you doing here?" I ran over to give her a hug, but then remembered that I shouldn't, and stopped just short of her wheelchair.

"What do you think?' Viviana managed to chuckle through her mask. I'm having a baby today!"

Alarmed, I could only think of whisking her safely to the maternity ward, away from stray viruses lurking in this very public place. I had hoped to get a couple hours of sleep before going into another long day. *Forget sleep! This is my little sister. And she needs me!* I practically ran, pushing Viviana in the wheelchair, and hurriedly pushed her chair onto an elevator. I entered, selected the fifth floor to the maternity ward, where a room was awaiting her.

Six long hours later, Viviana delivered a healthy baby boy. I stayed with her as much as I dared but had to leave her in the hands of another doctor. I returned to her side as soon as I found a five-minute window. I rushed into her room and found her with the baby in her arms. "You did it, Sis! What a beautiful baby boy you have!" I had to give the duo my distance, but looked on, grinning underneath my mask.

"Yes, I'm so happy, but very tired. I wish Tommy could see our little one."

"Soon. I heard you can go home tomorrow. Does the baby have a name yet? Did you and Tommy already talk about his name?"

"Yes, we already chose the name Jake. Tommy wants him to have more of an American name, since, you know, I'm Latina and he is Asian. We hope to live there eventually and raise the baby in California near Tommy's family."

"Very good. One day this whole pandemic will be in the past. You can tell your son all about it, and hope that we never have to go through one again." Viviana smiled at me, and a nurse came in at that moment to help her learn about nursing the baby. I took the cue, and left, saying I would check on her and the baby when I could.

Chapter 38

Cassie

October 2020

It was during a routine checkup exam that I was told the shattering news: Something was wrong, and I needed constant bedrest or face a possible miscarriage. "But doctor, how do I do that? I have a four-year-old and I live alone right now. My husband is working in Mexico. What can I do?" I peered up at Dr. Casey over my mask; he stared back at me over his own face covering, concern etched in his eyes.

"I realize this may be a huge inconvenience, but you will need to think about your situation and decide what you can do to help you reach full-term with this baby. Perhaps you have a relative who could come to stay? Is there a friend nearby or can you afford to hire some help? Each person handles this difficulty differently." Gently he helped me to a sitting position while I considered his words silently.

"I—I don't know what I can do yet," I replied slowly, still trying to process this new development. I thought of my options. There was Tully, but she would probably want me and Abbie to live with her in Springville. In that case, I would be far from Dr. Casey, six hours or so, and what if I needed to see him right away? Jasmine has her own two kids, plus teaches remotely from her home in

Springville. This too, didn't seem a possibility. Then I thought about Claire. She lived in San Francisco with Preston, but both were working remotely from their home. Would she want to stay up here with me, away from Preston for an indefinite time or until Luis returned?

Dr. Casey interrupted my reverie. "Well, think about it but not for too long—until tomorrow perhaps. After that, at least get something temporary going, like a babysitter for your child, and then arrange for a solution that is a bit more permanent. I can't emphasize it enough: your baby is in jeopardy until you get complete rest. You are on the older end of the scale for pregnancy, you know."

"Yes," I sighed, remembering my mother's advice to tell Luis about the baby before something like this happened. I had to let him know, regardless of our current noncommunication. Even if he is distracted with a patient—I must tell him. If I lost my baby before he even knew about it, things would become even more complicated and tense. Plus, it wasn't fair of me to keep this from him. "Thank you, Dr. Casey. I will go home and see what I can come up with."

"That's good, Cassie. Please call my receptionist later to let me know what you have arranged. Also, I'll need you to set up another appointment for a week from now, to see how things are progressing."

I stumbled out of the office, still in a daze at the disconcerting news, and wondering how and when to break everything to Luis. When I arrived back home, I phoned my editor, Sharon, to ask her if she knew of any temporary help—a babysitter or home health care worker—anyone really. I didn't know where to begin dealing with this new development. She promised that she would make inquiries and get back to me today or tomorrow.

As I unlocked the door to my house, Abbie raced ahead to find her favorite doll. I felt tired—drained of all energy. How do I tell Luis my news? Will he listen to me or interrupt me to care for a sick patient? I took a deep breath and opened the refrigerator to prepare lunch for Abbie and me. The call would have to wait for now.

After lunch, Abbie and I took a nap; the news was exhausting, and my body demanded rest. A couple of hours later or so, when I arose from my rest, I turned on the T.V. to distract my mind. How could it hurt to wait awhile before trying to contact Luis? It would just disappoint me when he didn't answer his phone. I didn't need more discouraging events today. It could wait. I didn't know who to contact next; the overwhelming fatigue made decisions seem unimportant. Abbie and I drifted along alone; only Dr. Casey and I knew about my serious condition. Frankly, I didn't care at this point. I was tired; exhausted with living alone with a small child and carrying one who was at risk.

Somehow, Abbie and I fell asleep together on my bed and we stayed there together the entire night. I slept fitfully, dreaming of the two of us, mother and child, strolling in the rain together. When I would rouse a bit, I snuggled into Abbie's warm little form, enjoying the little human nestled against me. Finally, around seven, I awakened to the nudging of Abbie. "Mommy, I'm hungry."

"Wh-what?" I felt disoriented at first; she had never slept the entire night with me before. "Yeah, I'll get up," I mumbled. Slowly, I dragged my tired body out of bed, and doused my face in cold water from the bathroom sink. I stumbled into the kitchen to start coffee and prepare Abbie's breakfast. I remembered then the doctor's warning to take better care of myself and made waffles for the two of us; actually, three of us, if I counted the little one awaiting to be born. It felt like it would be a long day ahead; the fatigue was taking its toll. Around nine, my editor, Sharon, called.

"Cassie, I found an adult babysitter who is willing to come in for a couple of hours a day for a week or two, until you get someone else. Are you interested?"

"Uh, I guess. I have to do something like right away."

"Okay. Her name is Sadie. I'll give you her number."

Sadie was ready to begin tomorrow, at ten in the morning, and stay until we had lunch, which she volunteered to prepare before leaving. After lunch, Abbie and I could take naps. It was a start, but I knew I would need much more. I wasn't supposed to clean the house or do laundry now with bedrest. But Sadie coming would give me more time to discover a better solution.

Chapter 39

CASSIE

"Of course! I'll fly up to stay with you, Girlfriend. You know I will."

"Oh, Claire, you're the best! Thanks so much."

"Well, that's what besties do. I'll just let Preston know, but he can fend for himself for a while. No problem. I'll check flights and see how soon I can come and bring my online work in my laptop."

The following Monday, Claire arrived at the Portland airport, and Abbie and I picked her up. I didn't know what else to do but make the trip myself. Claire insisted on driving my car back to Lincoln City, and I didn't protest. I was already very tired.

When we finally arrived back to our cottage in Lincoln City, I breathed a sigh of relief. I needed to lie down. Claire parked the car expertly, assisted Abbie, and opened the passenger door for me to slide out. I could hardly wait to take a nap but felt obliged to point out to Claire where household essentials were, along with food staples. "Okay, no worries. I will prepare something for dinner while you take a rest. I insist," Claire said, guiding me to my bedroom. It was then that I finally collapsed onto my bed and slept for two hours. I awoke to the aroma of spaghetti sauce simmering. I stumbled into the bathroom and splashed water on my face.

"Is that spaghetti that smells so delicious?" I padded into the kitchen, my nose alert to the pleasing aroma floating down the hall.

"Yes, and you can sit yourself down to the table here with Abbie. She is waiting patiently while I finish up."

"Mommy, I'm hungry. Aunt Claire is cooking for us, see?"

Claire smiled smugly, happy that Abbie referred to her as 'Aunt Claire'. "Yes, Sweetheart, your auntie is here to cook and clean while your mom gets the rest she needs, right?" Claire patted Abbie's frizzy head affectionately and returned to the stove to dish up a plate for each of us. A bowl of green salad awaited in the center of the table to round out the meal. I felt so helpless, yet grateful, with Claire preparing the dinner and cleaning up. She insisted I go into the living room while she cleared the table and put the dishes into the dishwasher. I sat on the sofa with Abbie, while she chattered on about her new Barbie doll that Claire had presented to her upon arriving. The doll came with a change of clothes, a pair of hiking shoes, pants and top, which Abbie repeatedly interchanged with the doll's original clothes, a lovely red cocktail dress. Absently, I nodded in agreement with whatever Abbie said, reflecting again about my lack of communication with Luis. I pondered how and when I would let him know my health situation and the coming baby.

CLAIRE JOINED ME IN THE LIVING ROOM AFTER TIDYING UP THE kitchen, plopping down on the sofa beside me. Abbie still played with her Barbie at the far end of the couch. "So, Girlfriend, have you talked to Luis yet?" Her eyes bored into mine, but her mouth turned up in a playful grin. I couldn't quite fathom why she would smile about something so serious for me as my tense relationship with Luis.

"Well, uh, not quite. I haven't felt up to it, you know. I'm basically tired or depressed or both all of the time I'm not sleeping."

"Alright. But don't wait too long, okay?"

"Easy for you to say. Let's change the subject for now. I am so exhausted from the drive into Portland and back. Maybe we could find a fun movie on T.V.? One Abbie might enjoy too?"

As it turned out, I fell asleep during the movie, *Frozen*. When I awakened, Claire had already put Abbie to bed, complete with Abbie's teeth brushed and pajamas on. So efficient, I realized. Gratefully, I crawled into my own bed, not bothering to put on pajamas or brush my teeth. Claire took to the couch to sleep on, first prowling around until she found a blanket and pillow. I fell into a fitful sleep, a dream repeating over and over again of a conversation I planned to have with Luis. In my dream, he became upset with me, refused to talk, and hung up the phone. In my dream, he decided to remain in Puebla for another year, not returning to see the new baby.

In the morning, Abbie joined me in bed and awakened me, but I felt disoriented and sad. The dream was having its effect. I couldn't seem to shake it off even after Abbie and I headed into the kitchen where Claire had started coffee.

Chapter 40

CASSIE

The new day dawned cold and overcast. Our town was already experiencing a cold snap—a bit unusual for the Oregon coast in early November. Claire was here with Abbie and me, so I wanted to feel happy, or at least, grateful, for Claire's company and help. Somehow, I couldn't shake off the dream. Was it real, or was I just imagining how Luis would react when I told him? I decided a walk would help me, and Claire bundled up Abbie and the three of us set out. We wandered down to the sand near the waves, and Abbie was excited.

"Mommie, look! A shell. Here, help me find more!" Her enthusiasm was contagious, and soon the three of us bent down, combing the shore for more. There never were many on the Northwestern Pacific coastline, but we managed to spot a few. Abbie soon resorted to retrieving pebbles, so much more prevalent on the Northwest beaches. Before long, she tired of the search, and ran off down the wet sand, chasing after a seagull. The waves rushed in, obscuring all sounds other than the roar of the ocean. It helped to block the bleak thoughts that insisted upon dominating my mind.

"Claire, do you think Luis will forgive me for not telling him about my news in a timely manner?" Claire walked closely beside me, as we tried to keep up with Abbie.

Claire hesitated before answering. "Oh, I'm certain it will be okay. He loves you, Cassie. But you need to tell him, don't you think?" Her eyes sparkled as she answered, which again seemed strange to me. It was only much later that I understood the reason.

We returned home for lunch, and then I collapsed again into an afternoon nap. Abbie, too, needed a nap, and Claire put her down in Abbie's bed. The house quieted, and Claire used the time to get onto her laptop to do online work for her job. When I awakened, again I smelled delicious cooking aromas coming from the kitchen. As I padded down the hall, I heard her humming as she worked. "What are we having? Smells delicious!"

"Oh, just some homemade chicken soup. My mother's recipe. Just sit yourself down while I finish up."

At that moment, Abbie rushed in. "Mommie, look! Barbie is going hiking today. Can we go too?"

"Not now, Sweetie. Aunt Claire is cooking dinner for us, and we'll eat soon. Another day, okay?"

"Oh. I want to go today. Humph! Barbie isn't going to be happy with that."

"I know. But Mommy isn't very strong to hike right now, remember?"

"Please can we go soon?" Abbie insisted, showing me her doll, dressed for a big excursion to the mountains.

"Someday, I promise." In my mind, that seemed highly unlikely, if ever, with a new baby on the horizon, plus my relationship in crisis with Luis.

Chapter 41

CASSIE

"So, Girlfriend, have you talked to Luis yet?" Claire asked yet again, the next morning over coffee. She looked up over her coffee mug, still a playful gleam in her eyes.

"Uh, no. I am so exhausted after dinner, and I seem to have things to do with Abbie during the day. It's just difficult, you know?" Nervously, I picked at my robe, discovering a speck of food on it. *I need to do a load of wash. Well, Claire will insist on doing the laundry.*

"Okay. But call soon, alright?" Again, she gave me an impish expression. I didn't care. I would call when I was up to it, physically and mentally. I felt defensive suddenly—and exhausted.

The day sped by, with me resting for a while in bed, then on the sofa, as I watched cartoons with Abbie. All too soon, it was dinnertime. Claire prepared a taco salad for the two of us, and hotdogs with fruit for Abbie. Today, I had very little appetite, but I made the effort to eat for the baby.

Eventually, I realized that I must do some reporting for the newspaper that employs me. Maybe next week I could ask Sharon for another feature story topic and attempt to do some writing while Abbie napped. Then I thought, *oh, right. Claire is here. It doesn't matter if Abbie is napping or not. Claire takes care of everything.*

I sighed and dosed off on the couch during the cartoons. Maybe I will feel better next week. I can always hope.

Early the next week, I assessed my situation. Claire had been extremely patient and understanding, but I could tell that she was becoming a little tired of it all. I just didn't improve, and I still had not contacted Luis. *Why does she want me to do that so badly?* She seemed to bring up the topic daily. I moped around each day, and Abbie was becoming a handful even for Claire. She needed more activity than Claire could provide, and Claire had all the chores of cooking and cleaning as well. I still avoided calling my editor for more work. I needed to feel stronger; I also needed to perk up my relationship with Luis, but I just didn't know how. Plus, it was only two weeks until Thanksgiving. What then? Will Claire return home to be with Preston? Will it be just Abbie and me for the day? The idea sent me into another downward spiral. I was afraid to ask Claire yet.

Chapter 42

TULLY

NOVEMBER 20, 2020
BUTTERFLY SANCTUARY, MEXICO

Me! Getting married again! Robert and I were making wedding plans. I still couldn't believe it, so I didn't tell Jasmine or Cassie, or any of the family yet. I had to be certain of the how and when. I debated on how to break the news to them; after all, they still grieved their father, Sean. The funny thing is that Cassie's real father is Robert, so she should be very happy about it, but one never knew the heart and mind of children in a given situation. Thanksgiving was just around the corner, so Robert and I thought that, if possible, we would make the trip to Seattle after Thanksgiving and tell them. Perhaps we could remain in the area through Christmas and have the wedding during the holidays. The problem was the Pandemic. We weren't sure how that would play out.

The wedding would have to be small and simple. Washington and Oregon were still under restrictions for large group gatherings. The media discouraged even family gatherings, due to the spread of the virus. Masking was also still a mandate. Somehow, we would try to pull it off. Inwardly, I felt excitement building at the prospect of getting married to Robert. He exuded warmth, love, and kindness. I truly did love him.

As an older woman, not my first, young, go-round with marriage, I daydreamed of what to wear for the wedding. I wouldn't be able to shop, really, unless I trusted online shopping, which was out of the question up here on the mountain. We only had online access in town, and it would be too difficult to shop online and choose something so important as a bridal dress while using the local pharmacy computer. I thought back to my wardrobe at home, and mentally chose a mint green sheath that I once wore to a special business dinner with my former husband, Sean. No one would remember the dress anyway. It looked chic, complementing my figure, but at the same time, it was modest. Yes, that would have to do. I owned a pair of black pumps that I wore with it before, so I was all set. I imagined carrying a beautiful bouquet of white calla lilies, but where I could acquire that was unknown, since things were still limited due to the Pandemic. I would have to discover what was available after we arrived in Washington.

"Do you think this will be good for the wedding?" Robert held up a black suit, an expensive cut from the looks of it, complete with a white dress shirt and green tie. "I wore it to Cassie's wedding, if you remember."

"Oh, right! That looks perfect to me." I touched the fabric, which felt like luxurious silk.

"Yeah, I'll look handsome for you, I hope." He grinned, replacing it in the closet. "Now I must focus on getting ready to leave here for a while. I know I'll need to return sometime after the wedding and honeymoon to pack up. Jose will be going off to the university, and eventually come back to take my place in the Monarch research."

"I'm so glad you have arranged for Jose to take over. You'll be able to retire, right?"

"Well, I suppose so. I'll be up in Washington enjoying life with you in your place." Robert grinned mischievously, patting my bottom gently.

The next day, Jose brought up two horses for us, and we headed down to the town. While there, we did an online search to see the status of the Pandemic in Washington and Oregon. It appeared that the lockdown had been lifted, but a mask mandate was in place. In some cases, there was a limit to how many people could congregate in one venue, such as churches. Schools were still online. Our decision to hold our wedding at Jasmine's and limit it to a few close family members seemed to be a good one. At this point in our lives, we didn't really want a large gig anyway. I would ask Jasmine to work on the details for food and decorations, which I also wanted to keep simple. I hoped that Jasmine could find someone to officiate. The date was still a bit uncertain, but we would let her know about our plans soon.

Chapter 43

CASSIE

I still couldn't bring myself to call Luis. What was my excuse now? I suppose I would have to say that I was just discouraged, depressed, and yes, a little resentful. Maybe a whole lot resentful. After all, he didn't seem to care about what was going on with Abbie and me. Did he care? Only Claire seemed to think so. She still gave me that sly half grin whenever she mentioned the suggestion to call him. I just shrugged, and then either took a nap or watched T.V. I realized that I was suffering from depression and fatigue. Actually, the fatigue was mostly physical, since my complication of pregnancy required me to rest. As Thanksgiving drew near, Claire occasionally brought it up. What would we have for the day? A turkey? It seemed a bit much for a sick pregnant woman and young child. So, we did nothing to prepare for the day.

"Are you returning to San Francisco to be with Preston for Thanksgiving?" I felt totally selfish with Claire here and Preston alone at Claire's home.

"Oh, don't worry about Preston. He has a large family. He'll just join in at his parents' house with his siblings. No problem. I decided to stay here with you."

"So then, we need to fix something festive. How about a turkey breast? That isn't so large for the three of us."

Claire gave me that curious smile again. "Sure. Sounds good. I'll look for one on my next trip out to the store, okay?"

Now it was three days until Thanksgiving. Claire brought out the construction paper for Abbie, and the two of them created turkeys with their hands as patterns. Abbie seemed to enjoy the activity and made several in different colors. "Look, Mommie! I made one for you and one for Daddy, and also for me and Claire. See?" As I observed her creations, I felt a catch form in my throat. Where was Luis? Was he truly Abbie's Dad anymore, or just a doctor working for others in a foreign country? What about us?

"Yes, I see. Those are very nice, Abbie. Want to put them on the refrigerator or tape them to the window for others to see?" I tried very hard to smile, glad that Claire had engaged her in this art activity. I gave Claire a grateful smile and reached out to hold Abbie. She scampered off, not allowing my touch.

"Put them on the window. I want Daddy to see when he comes home." Abbie grabbed the paper turkeys, handing them to Claire to mount on the window by the front door.

"Sure, Honey. Let's do it. Maybe Daddy will see them soon," Claire replied, again giving me a strange look. I took a deep breath, slightly annoyed at their charades with Luis returning home. *Why give Abbie a false hope? Additionally, why should I have hope? He didn't care about what was going on up here anyway.*

Chapter 44

CASSIE

"God didn't give up on me. I am somebody in God's eyes... Let me be a prime example of how I've been through the storm and the rain, and I made it over."

—Fantasia Barrino

The days slipped by quickly, and soon, it was Thanksgiving. Claire slid the turkey breast into the oven by ten o'clock that morning, and we sipped coffee, munching on Danish pastries she had picked up at the grocery. I felt glum and a bit sad, although grateful not to be spending the day alone with only Abbie and me. The pastries helped cheer my heart a bit.

Suddenly, there was a soft knock on the door. "Who could that be on Thanksgiving morning?" I asked. "Don't answer until you look out the window to see who it is," I cautioned. Claire and Abbie obediently scampered over to the window and looked out.

"It's Daddy!" Abbie shrieked in delight. "I knew he would be here to see his paper turkey!"

Claire turned to give me a grin, as if to say, "I told you," and jerked open the door. As Luis entered, he appeared taller and more handsome to me than I remembered and scooped up Abbie into his arms. Claire quickly gave him a side hug. He just stood there in the entrance a moment, not sure of what to do next. I remained in the kitchen doorway, an unsightly spectacle with my frizzy hair standing on end, wearing a pink bathrobe, my pregnant stomach protruding. I was still clutching my cup of coffee in front of me like a shield, not allowing myself to move or speak. Luis remained motionless, still holding Abbie, staring at me as if awaiting permission to acknowledge me. I stared back, speechless. I was too shocked to know what else to do.

It was Claire who finally broke the ice. "Go on, Luis. Cassie is here, waiting for you." By this time, Abbie had squirmed her way out of Luis' grasp, heading for the paper turkeys on the window. She grabbed one, pulling off the tape that held it fast to the window.

"Here, Daddy. I made this one for you," Abbie proclaimed, handing him a brown construction paper turkey with red feathers glued on.

"Thank you, Sweetheart," Luis answered, reaching down to accept the turkey, but not taking his eyes off me. I stood, like a huge, fat, pink flamingo, willing myself to move, but motionless, still clinging to the cup of coffee. Claire had backed away, clearing a path for Luis and me to meet, but neither of us took the first step. We just stood there, a moment in time, transfixed, as statues. I was afraid to breathe, not wanting to appear as a real, functioning human. I willed myself to be a strong lioness, knowing full well that I wasn't.

Too much time elapsed. Outside, the rain kept up its steady fall, audible on the windowpanes and roof. The clock ticked away, marking the time in the living room; I was aware of the sound, as if it were my heart, beating for all to hear. Luis held onto the paper turkey, nearly gripping it hard enough to tear it. "Daddy, do you want to put it back on the window?" Abbie held his hand, as Luis released it for her to take the artwork from him. Still, he didn't break his gaze upon me. I, the puffy flamingo in the fleece bathrobe, felt like I was in the crosshairs of a rifle.

"Sure, Sweetheart, let Claire help you tape it onto the window again," Luis said absently.

Claire sprang into action, relieved to be able to do something ordinary. "Help me, Abbie. Where do you want it this time?" Abbie scampered to the window with Claire, and busily they arranged all the turkeys on the glass once more. It was an attempt at normalcy in the midst of awkwardness.

As Luis continued his unrelenting stare at me, he finally said, "You didn't call. You didn't tell me."

My reply dried in my mouth; I couldn't speak. My voice went mute; sawdust replaced saliva. Tears formed in my eyes instead. I dropped the cup on the floor, weeping on the spot where I stood. I was aware of the breaking sound. As I bent down to retrieve the broken mug, audibly sobbing, Luis crouched down to the floor with me, picking up the shards. He took my arm and helped me up, guiding me to the sofa, and we slowly lowered ourselves down onto the cushions together. "Let's clean this up later. Sit with me, okay?" Luis still held my gaze, this time with the tenderness in his eyes I remembered so well.

Time continued to stand still, although the clock in the living room continued to click away the moments. The rain continued to fall softly outside. Claire coaxed Abbie into her bedroom to play with her Barbie to give us some space to talk. Neither Luis nor I wanted to be the first to speak. We were strangers—apart for months, filling our lives with the hurt and anger of isolation, of misunderstanding. It had been an eon of time for me: coping alone during the Pandemic with a young child and a difficult pregnancy. Through it all, Luis didn't know or seem to care. He was off in another country, so different from here in culture and way of thinking. Suddenly, I realized that none of that mattered now. It all faded and withered to a dried husk. He was here. His eyes spoke of love that had never dimmed with the passing of our separation. I could see that now.

"You returned to the rain at last. And to Abbie and me." I choked on the last phrase and wept openly.

Wordlessly, he put his arm around me as we sat close on the sofa. I leaned in, my head resting on his shoulder. "Claire called me," was all he said. He whispered the statement into my ear, and it was all I needed to know.

There was so much to say, yet nothing at all. Where would we begin? What was it I had yearned to tell him for all the past months? It didn't matter now. It was hard to wrap my mind around the idea. I didn't need to give him the speech I had mentally rehearsed over and over: the news of the coming child and the plea to beg him to come home. He was here now and could see my bulging stomach for himself. I was due to give birth in less than two months. That is, if all went well. How could it not? Luis was home at last. Now my tears of fear and uncertainty had turned to happiness and relief.

Chapter 45

CASSIE

"I've always found the rain very calming."
—Venus Williams

Claire's job was accomplished here in our home; she departed the day after Thanksgiving for the airport to return to the San Francisco area. Both Luis and I thanked her many times. Not only did she fly up here to assist Abbie and me, leaving Preston and her own home, she had contacted Luis to urge him to return home to me. "No worries, Girlfriend. That's what we do as friends. We'll be in touch." Little did I know how soon I would see Claire again.

With Luis returning, it wasn't long before we got into a new routine. Each day, the three of us took strolls along the beach, and often, in the rain. We all loved the rain, gently caressing our faces and hair. Luis took two weeks to get Abbie and me situated before going back to his medical practice here in Lincoln City. During the time he had been gone, his partners at the local clinic had taken on his patients. Now they, too, could get back to a new normal, practicing medicine during the pandemic with just their own patients. Since he had returned, I visited Dr. Casey, to see if I could manage Abbie by myself during the hours Luis was in the clinic. I felt a bit stronger than before; Dr. Casey was cautiously optimistic but advised me to nap while Abbie took hers and then watch T.V. or read until Luis came home to prepare dinner. Luis approached the added responsibility with enthusiasm. He was glad to be here and be a part of our lives once more.

Before we realized it, Christmas was fast approaching. Abbie was excited with anticipation. The feeling was contagious, and I, too, looked forward to it. The baby would arrive after the holiday, in early January. With Luis here at last, it would be a Christmas to remember.

Chapter 46

TULLY

Robert and I had planned our wedding before I left to return to Washington. He, of course, continued to live on the mountain in Mexico, but was arranging to travel here in mid-December. Jose would travel with him to the wedding. In the meantime, he had to not only prepare to come up here, but also help Jose to be ready to take over for him. Eventually, Jose would live in the cabin, but first had to study entomology at the university.

The wedding would be very simple, really. We would hold it at Jasmine's, and with only our close family and a few friends. I opened my closet and pulled out my green sheath dress, to make sure it still fit. I had lost a little weight since living in Mexico for those months there. I looked at myself in the mirror; the dress would do. I still hoped for the white calla lilies to carry but I knew I would probably have to settle for something else. It didn't matter. Robert and I decided on getting married on the day after Christmas, December 26. It would be simpler that way.

Jasmine oversaw securing the officiant for the wedding. She also planned to order my bouquet as well as a floral arrangement to be displayed in her living room. Food was another matter. We decided to have appetizers and of course, a cake. Jasmine's husband,

John, would pick those up from a caterer, unless they were willing to make the delivery during this ongoing pandemic.

Robert and I decided to wait until the pandemic passed before going on an official honeymoon. I felt like we had already had one anyway, with my extended visit in Mexico. One day, things would look better to be out and about.

Cassie didn't know our plans yet. We hoped to surprise her with the news when she drove up with Luis on Christmas. She needed to focus on her and the baby's health. I was sure that she would be excited about our upcoming event. I could hardly wait!

Chapter 47

CASSIE

"Abbie, would you like a baby sister?" Abbie and I were reading a story together about a baby foal. It seemed as good a time as any to approach the subject of a baby with Abbie. She hadn't asked me anything yet, even though my stomach was pooching out larger and larger with the passing of time.

Abbie glanced up from the picture book of the baby horse, staring at me. "Well, Mommy, will she play Barbie with me?" My heart sank a bit. That wasn't quite the response I was going for.

"Not for a while. She has to grow bigger first. Babies are small."

"Grow big like me? Then no—I don't want a sister." Abbie turned the page of the book with a flourish, finished with our little discussion. Her face appeared resolute and unconcerned.

"Well, you could hold a baby sister, like a baby doll—at least, for a minute, maybe," I added hastily, suddenly fearful that a young child might drop a baby.

"I'll think about it. Maybe if I have to have a baby sister I can decide then." Abbie continued to turn the pages, asking me to finish reading the baby horse story. The idea of a baby sister held little importance for her.

Later that day, Abbie and I went out for a walk. I had done little of that since my required bedrest. I was feeling restless and had a little more energy. It would be okay. As we ambled around the neighborhood, suddenly I felt a twinge in my abdomen. "Abbie, I think we better head back. Mommy is tired now."

"I don't want to go home yet," she declared. "I want to walk down by the beach."

"Okay, but not far," I relented. As we ventured down to the public beach access, the twinge grew more intense. "Abbie, we have to go back now," I insisted. We turned around, and I began a faster pace, holding onto Abbie and forcing her to trot to keep up. Before reaching our house, I remembered that I had brought my cell phone. I left a message for Luis, who was probably seeing a patient at the moment. By the time he called me back, we were nearing the walkway to our house.

"Cassie, can you comfortably get into the house, or do you need me to come right away?" Luis sounded more worried than I felt, so I assured him I could make it just fine. He remained on the line to be certain I was alright. But I wasn't. The twinge turned into a strong contraction, to where I had difficulty breathing. Luis detected the difficulty. "Cass, I'm calling for an ambulance. I'll see you in Emergency. No argument."

The ambulance reached us within minutes. Paramedics loaded me onto a stretcher, lifting me inside and whisked Abbie and me to emergency. I felt a bit ridiculous having to lie down on the stretcher but complied. Abbie looked on in fear, but the paramedic gave her a stuffed bear toy to play with until we arrived. Luis arrived shortly after. He joined me in the cubicle the emergency room afforded, and held my hand, his face anxious. "What if this had happened while I was far away in Mexico, and didn't even know you were pregnant? What then? It scares me, Cassie."

"Well, you are here now, when it counts." I gave him a wan smile, feeling the contractions even then, as I lay in the hospital bed. I was hooked up to monitors that checked my heart as well as the heart of the baby. Abbie sat on a chair, not sure what to do. At least Luis was here. He took over, lifting Abbie onto his lap in the chair. Truly, I felt so grateful for his presence here. How did I ever think I could do all of this alone, with possible complications?

After two hours or so the pain subsided, and the tests that were run in emergency proved to be in the normal range. I was released to go home, if I remained resting at home for the remainder of the day. The bedrest instructions were renewed, as my personal doctor was contacted. He wanted me to come into his office in a week for follow-up. Meekly, I did what was required. No more outings alone with Abbie for now.

"Okay Cassie, I trust that you will do as you were instructed, and rest for the few hours until I get back home. Okay? Abbie will need a nap anyway. When I get home, we will think about dinner."

"Of course. I will be good, no worry." Again, I offered a weak smile of reassurance, or at least I hoped it would be assuring. Luis gave me a peck on the cheek and went back to his office. Abbie and I could use a nap at this point in the action filled day.

Chapter 48

TULLY

As Christmas rapidly approached, I prepared for my departure from Robert's mountain cabin in Mexico. It was easier now to obtain a flight back to the States, so I had a reservation for two days from now. Robert was to meet me at the Seattle airport in three days, along with Jose. Jose arriving was also a surprise—Cassie was not expecting him to arrive for Christmas. I was getting excited and nervous. It would be our first Christmas together as a couple, as well as blending our families together over the holidays. Plus, of course, the big event for us would be our wedding the day after.

Since Jasmine was hosting the celebration, she oversaw nearly all of the details of the wedding. When I returned to Springville, I would hastily prepare for our Christmas as a family at my condo. My stomach felt jumpy at the thought of my flight, Christmas at my house, and most of all, the wedding. Would Cassie approve? We were keeping it a secret from her so that she wouldn't try to help get it ready. Rest was more important for her.

"Jasmine, I was able to call you today since I'm down in the village. How is everything going? Does Cassie know? Is she suspicious of our plans?"

"Everything is fine, Mom. Don't worry. Just get up here, okay?" Jasmine chuckled, her voice reassuring for me. My stomach quit turning over for the minutes we talked on the phone. Soon I would be there, and the final details would take shape. At least, that's what Jasmine said. "And no, Cassie doesn't suspect a thing. We are just discussing Christmas dinner, gifts, and all that."

"Is she resting enough, do you think?"

"Well, I'm not with her, but she claims that she is. I insist that she leave all the Christmas planning up to you and me, so she is trying not to get too involved. Little does she know what else we have up our sleeves, right?" Jasmine laughed, awaiting my answer.

"Right, right. I just hope she will be okay with this surprise wedding idea." I was worrying too much but couldn't seem to help myself. Here I was, atop a remote mountain in Mexico, in a crude cabin, planning to marry, unbeknownst to Cassie, her biological father. I had to admit it was a bit reckless for my age.

Jasmine read my mind. "Quit worrying, Mom. You deserve to be happy, and Robert is a great guy. I like him—I'm certain Cassie will be thrilled."

"Have you informed Claire of the plans, and invited her and Preston?"

"All done. She will be there in time for the wedding. No worries. She is excited and will keep our little secret, too."

"Well then. I will see all of you soon. Thank you, my younger daughter. Love you."

"You too, Mom. See you soon."

SOON, MY FLIGHT LANDED IN SEATTLE, WHERE JASMINE'S husband, John, picked me up and drove back to Springville. I had two days to prepare for Christmas at my house, after being absent for two months. I had no idea how I would purchase and prepare the dinner as well as decorate in time before everyone arrived. As I unlocked the door to my condo, John stood aside with my luggage, grinning. As I entered, there in the living room stood a fully decorated tree, with gifts already under it. I gasped. "Oh my! What a wonderful surprise! John, did you know about this?"

"Sure. Jasmine and I did it. Look in your refrigerator." I pulled open the refrigerator door, and it was stocked with essentials, including a large ham. John continued grinning.

I gave John a huge hug. "Oh, John. This is the best present ever! How can I thank you? I really didn't know how I would pull off Christmas here and my wedding the following day." Tears of gratitude flowed down my cheeks.

"Think nothing of it, except to say we're so glad to have you home. Rest up from your trip and we'll see you soon!" With that, he gave me a parting side hug and left.

After I was alone, I realized how tired I was, and snuggled up with Sebastian and Mandy, my cats. Both meowed and circled around my legs over and over. They had missed me terribly, as had I them. Jasmine and her children came each day to care for them, so they were okay, but missing me. The three of us took a long nap on my bed. There would be time tomorrow to check all my food supplies and begin preliminary preparations for Christmas dinner, which was just two days away.

Chapter 49

CASSIE

"Mommy, will Santa Claus know where to bring my toys at Grandma's? I don't want him to skip me." Abbie looked into my eyes imploring me to answer.

"Of course. He knows where you will be Christmas Eve. Don't worry." I tussled Abbie's hair with my hand as we snuggled together in bed. We had to wait for Luis to get home, and then the next morning, make our journey up to Washington to Tully's house.

"And Grandma doesn't' have a chimney. How will Santa get in?" Abbie insisted.

"Don't worry about that either, little one. He finds a way in. You can set out cookies and milk, too. He will like that." Whew! This Santa fantasy was sometimes tenuous, at least for a precocious child, which Abbie certainly was.

It was December 23. We planned to drive up ahead of Christmas day. Most of my gift shopping had to be done online this year, due to the Pandemic. Plus, it was a must for me in my condition. I had purchased gifts for everyone, including Jasmine's family, of course, and Tully. I had even remembered to buy my adopted grandmother, Vicki, a gift of warm gloves. Abbie was hoping for a Barbie house, which Luis and I planned to give her as her Santa present. Luis packed the car without Abbie's inquisitive eyes, while I occupied her with breakfast. She would most certainly ask about the large bags of presents, especially the Barbie house.

Soon we set off with Luis behind the wheel. He drove cautiously, the precious cargo of his family tucked in and belted securely. As he drove, he glanced anxiously over to where I sat in the passenger seat, giving me a half grin. "Don't worry, Luis. I feel fine. It will be good to see Jasmine's family and Mom. I'm okay, really.!"

"I know, I know. Just checking. It's a vocational hazard as a doctor sometimes. Especially when it comes to my own pregnant wife." Luis looked in his rear-view mirror. "Abbie, are you doing okay back there?"

"Yes, Daddy. I'm just holding my Barbie that Aunt Claire gave me. Barbie wanted to go too. But she doesn't have a car seat. Can I get one for her?"

Luis chuckled. "We'll have to look for that sometime, little one. Just be patient. It is a six-hour drive to Grandma's."

We stopped for a quick lunch near Portland, and then continued our journey, arriving at Tully's around five o'clock. I felt exhausted, and immediately went to Tully's spare bedroom to lie down. Sebastian and Mandy had already claimed the bed, as cats will do. Sebastian didn't care that I was lying down on the bed with him, but Mandy scuttled underneath the bed. It had truly been a long day for me. I could hear Tully and Luis in the background as I lay there, their conversation lulling me to sleep. I didn't notice until I awakened that Abbie had fallen asleep next to me, her Barbie still clutched in her hands. Luis came in and awakened the two of us for a dinner of spaghetti, my favorite at Tully's.

Chapter 50

CASSIE

Christmas came and went —in the evening, I sat on Tully's sofa afterward, sipping a mug of peppermint tea. I felt exhausted but content. I was thankful that we would sleep here once more at Tully's since I had zero energy to go anywhere else. Jasmine and her family had departed for their home but before she left, I noticed a sly, secretive glance from her to Tully. Tully had returned the same look. *What were they up to?* I was too tired to care, really, and settled back into the cushion, holding my comforting beverage, as Abbie sat on the floor playing with her new Ken doll. Now Barbie had a companion. I breathed deeply, enjoying the peace of the evening after the unwrapping frenzy was over. Luis helped Tully clean up the aftermath of wrapping paper and plates and cups. As I took a sip of tea, there was a knock on the front door.

"Oh good! That will be Robert." Tully strode over to the door, peeking through the eye hole before opening.

"Robert is here? I didn't know he was coming." I glanced over to the door, wondering why Tully hadn't mentioned that my dad was flying up.

Tully ignored my question, swinging open the door. "Robert!

Welcome! Merry Christmas!" Tully embraced Robert, who swiftly kissed her on the lips.

"Merry Christmas, Tully." Robert stepped in, then saw the rest of us in the living room. "Merry Christmas, everyone! Sorry I'm late." He grinned then at his attempt at a joke.

"I didn't know you were joining us, but welcome, Robert—Dad!" I didn't get up; the fatigue was taking its toll.

"Stay where you are. No worries. Yes, I was to be the Christmas evening surprise. Did it work?" Robert looked from one to another, grinning, and grabbing Tully around the waist. I noticed that Luis looked smug—almost satisfied to see Robert. I couldn't quite make it all out. *What is going on? Everyone but me seems to be in on a secret.*

"All right. I may have to take frequent rest breaks, but I'm not oblivious. What is going on? Did I miss something?" I gazed from Tully to Luis to Robert. All were wearing the same little smirk on their faces. I saw Tully and Robert look into one another's eyes, and then nod.

Tully took a deep breath before speaking. "Yes, Cassie. Sorry. We didn't want to stress you out further. We know that coming up here to Springville was a big ordeal, as well as being a part of all of the Christmas festivities today. But…"

"What Tully is trying to get at is that we are getting married tomorrow!" Robert blurted out. Everyone seemed to let out a collective sigh, relieved that someone finally revealed the mystery.

"What? Why didn't I get to know? What the heck?" I felt foolish to be on the outside of what everyone else must have known for some time.

"Tully just tried to explain why. We have all been trying to protect you and the baby. But we're here, and there will be a wedding tomorrow!" Luis put his arm around my shoulders, and

I couldn't help myself. I teared up a little, happy to realize what was soon transpiring.

"Oh my! So, my real dad is marrying my adopted mom! What a Christmas gift!" I looked from one to another, in utter amazement. I never imagined this really happening, although I dreamed of it. In actuality, I was the one who brought them together by searching and finding my real father. "Where will this take place?"

"At Jasmine's." Tully appeared at peace and took Robert's hand. "That's why she scooted out a bit early. There's a lot to get ready."

At that moment, the phone rang. Tully answered and handed me the phone. It was Claire. She and Preston had arrived at Jasmine's and were busy helping her set up. There will be a wedding in the morning! Who knew? I was still tired, but excited as well. I hoped that the news of my father and adopted mother getting married wouldn't keep me up.

I had nothing to worry about. As soon as my head hit the pillow, I fell into a blissful sleep. Sometimes, dreams do come true.

Chapter 51

CASSIE

"I love the ending of a movie where two people end up together. Preferably if there's rain and an airport or running or a confession of love."

—Taylor Swift

December 26, 2020, dawned cold and rainy. I slept well, which was a good thing, with the full day ahead. I awakened, at first not sure of where I was. Then I recognized Tully's second bedroom and noticed that Luis had already gotten up. *The wedding! Right!* I tried to get up from bed too quickly and had to sit on the edge for a moment. What was I going to wear? I had nothing suitable for a wedding and was nearly nine months pregnant. Nothing would fit anyway. I'd just have to wear my casual pregnant clothes that I had brought. I opened my suitcase, rummaging around, tossing things aside. I did remember to bring a somewhat nice top, in a blue chiffon. It flowed out around my stomach but looked okay. *Yes, that would have to do, along with a pair of black maternity slacks.*

I donned my bathrobe and waddled into the bathroom to use the toilet and splashed water on my face. "There you are my love!

"Come into the kitchen and get a bite of breakfast," Luis said, taking my arm and leading me into the kitchen.

"I know where the kitchen is, Luis," I protested, giggling. As I nibbled on toast and sipped some orange juice, my phone rang.

"Hey, Girlfriend, it's Claire. Can you believe it? Preston and I are here in Springville to help with your mom's wedding! You heard by now, right?"

"Uh, yes, I'm glad you all finally let me in on the scheme. You guys conspired against me." I chuckled but let her know in an offhand way that she went a little behind my back.

"I know, I know. We felt that we had to do it that way. And you and the baby are here, and doing fine, right?"

"Well, yes. We are—sure. Just big and pregnant. No pretty wedding clothes, but I will be there. I wouldn't miss it—my adopted mom and my real dad. I still have to pinch myself to believe it's happening!"

"Don't pinch too hard. Might upset the baby, you know!" Claire tittered, as if she worried that I was upset with her for keeping the secret so well.

"Right, right. Don't worry. I feel fine this morning. Guess I'll see you soon. At the wedding!"

It was already eight in the morning, and the wedding was to be at eleven. I looked out the window to see a fine drizzle of rain. Just three short hours. I suddenly remembered that Abbie needed something appropriate to wear as well. I got up, juice in hand, to prowl through Abbie's clothes. As I was throwing one thing after another out onto the bed, Luis joined me. "How would this look?" He was holding up Abbie's pink frilly dress, something I had purchased on a whim a couple of months ago.

"Perfect! How did it get here to Tully's house?" I smiled, snatching it from Luis, touching the lacey scallops that rimmed the edges.

"Oh, just a bit of last-minute magic. I put it in my overnight bag to surprise you. Will it be okay for her, do you think?" Luis looked at me mischievously, pleased with himself to have remembered it.

"Oh, yes!" I gave him a hug, summoning Abbie to the bedroom, to hold it up to her.

"I can wear it today, right, Mommy?" Abbie jumped up and down, excited to have a place to wear such a dress. "It's like a Barbie dress! Can I bring her to the wedding too?"

"Of course. Grandma won't mind at all, I'm sure."

Luis had brought his grey suit, complete with a green shirt and tie. He would look handsome, as always. Then there was me—nine months pregnant, slacks and top. *Oh well. It would have to do. The wedding wasn't about me.* Two and a half hours rushed by, and all too soon, it was time to go to Jasmine's for the big event. Tully looked elegant in her green sheath dress; her auburn hair was swept up in a chignon at the nape of her neck. Later, at the ceremony, Jasmine added a small but glittery tiara to Tully's lovely copper-colored hair.

The day continued with misty rain, typical of the area at this time of year. Jasmine's house was only an eight-minute drive, and Luis loaded all of us in, driving carefully. The windshield wipers were the only sound as Luis wound his car through the streets. We would meet up with Robert and the rest at Jasmine's. I wasn't certain who all would be there, but I would soon find out.

Chapter 52

CASSIE

When we arrived with the bride, all the other family members and friends were seated and waiting for the ceremony to begin. The living room was set up with extra chairs, and we were greeted with the fragrance of gardenias, mixed in with cala lilies, Tully's flowers of choice. She would carry a small bouquet of the same flowers which also graced the table where the vows would take place. All heads turned to look as we made our entrance. Evidently, everyone but me had known early on that this was happening. Robert, of course, was there to take Tully by the hand, ushering her to two seats in the front. He appeared tall, dark, and handsome in his well-cut black suit, seeming totally at ease with the event about to take place.

Jasmine and John and their two children, Josh and Josie, dashed around in the kitchen, arranging napkins and plates, and preparing the refreshments for later. I wished that I could help out, but Luis had already seated me in a chair. As I looked around the room, I made a mental note of who was there. My grandma, Vicki, was seated next to Uncle Luke and his wife, Amy, and their son, Thomas. There was Claire and Preston, of course, who were also bustling around in the kitchen with Jasmine's family. I saw a man wearing a clerical collar, no doubt the officiant for the wedding. Off to the side, there he was: Jose, the horseback tour guide from the Monarch Sanctuary, my **brother.** My real brother. "Luis, I need to greet someone." I got up before Luis could object and made my way to where Jose was sitting. "Oh, Jose! I know now that you are my brother! I had wanted to visit you on the mountain but received a ticket to return home before I could talk to you. I never got the chance until now." Tears rose in my eyes—I couldn't help myself. Quickly he stood and gave me a comforting embrace—the first of many, I hoped.

"It's okay, Sis. I only learned that I had a sister just a short time ago, too. But here I am, your brother for life!" Jose chuckled, then went on. "Now, I also see that I'm going to become an uncle soon." Jose grinned at me affectionately, hugging me once more. "Let's chat and do some catching up after the wedding, okay, Sis?"

"Yes! Absolutely." I took his hand and gave it a squeeze. I could tell that Jose enjoyed calling me "Sis." I liked the sound of the word as well. "I don't want to stop talking. This is so wonderful to share our father's wedding. Later then." I returned to my seat with Luis and Abbie, a little shaken, but elated.

"Mommy, who is that man?" Abbie whispered after I sat down. She turned around to stare at Jose.

"He's your Uncle Jose," I replied happily.

"I didn't know I had an uncle," Abbie whispered back. "Except for Uncle Luke, but he is your uncle too."

"Right. Uncle Jose is my brother, Abbie." I smiled to myself at the thought. To think that my real brother was here to see Tully married—almost too much to contemplate. It was truly the culmination of my dreams of home.

The wedding went off smoothly, and as everyone was mingling and eating finger food and wedding cake, I felt a strange sensation. "Luis, I think my water just broke." I grabbed his arm, interrupting his conversation with Jose.

"What? It's three weeks early, isn't it?" Luis looked over to me in alarm.

"Y—yes, it is. Nevertheless, I think it may be happening. What do we do?" My eyes must have been huge, and Luis became even more visibly anxious.

"Well, we say goodbye and head to the nearest hospital." Luis took Tully aside for a moment, asking her for the location of the nearest hospital, although he also began searching the G.P.S. on his phone. As quietly as possible, we made our exit, leaving Abbie with Jasmine.

Five hours later, on the same day as my adopted mother and biological father's wedding, baby Amalia made her entrance into the world and into our family. It was an unimaginable finish to a perfect day for me: the surprise wedding, meeting up with my brother, and Amalia's arrival as a healthy baby girl of six pounds. Returning to the land of rain had fulfilled my wildest of dreams.

Epilogue
CASSIE

JUNE 2023

"Wisdom is like the rain. Its source is limitless, but it comes down according to the season."

—*Rumi*

Tully and Robert had decided against a honeymoon, Tully proclaiming that they had had enough of "exotic locations." Her wedding on December 26, 2021, started off smoothly, despite the fact that it was held in Jasmine's home because of the ongoing pandemic. Did I say started off smoothly? Toward the end of the ceremony, unborn baby Amalia decided to make her entrance into the world. Luis had to drop everything and rush me to a nearby hospital, so Amalia was born in Springville, Washington, instead of near our home in Lincoln City, Oregon.

Now, Amalia is two years old, and Abbie, her big sister, age six. Abbie would start first grade in the fall. I reflected on this as Luis and I sat on our deck, sipping coffee from our mugs, and watching the two girls play in the sand of our beachfront bungalow.

Our small beach house was an inheritance that Dr. Jordan had bequeathed to me. He had been the one who helped me to find my father so many years ago now.

Even though it was early June, a soft mist fell from the overhead clouds. The girls didn't mind; busily they dug in the sand, creating roadways for Abbie's Barbie car. They were wearing matching yellow raincoats and hats, along with pink rain boots.

The waves lapped at the sand further down on the public beach, their methodical rhythm lulling me back into my memories. At my feet romped our newest addition, our little gray male kitty we named Domino, in honor of our old, now deceased cat, Dominican, who once belonged to Dr. Jordan. Domino was wrestling with my shoelaces, still very playful at only two years of age.

"You know, Luis, when I was eighteen and left home to visit my biological mom, I never envisioned how my life could become so rich with family. I have not only my adopted family, but my father, Robert, my brother, Jose, you, and our two girls, and even a cat. After all my travels in search of my father, I never thought I would discover so much. Even my good friends, Claire, Preston, and Tommy, are all a part of my life because of my quest to find my father. Then I met you and your family. Returning to the Northwest rain has ended my journey—and I'm so content. What more could I ever ask for?"

"Nothing, I guess. Just don't ever stop loving me." Luis took my arm as we sat on our deck chairs and squeezed my hand gently.

"No chance of that. You're here with me, and that's all I'll ever need," I answered, smiling into his eyes.

Acknowledgments

I would like to thank Marlene Loisdotter for her invaluable expertise, encouragement, and editing advice. Her ongoing inspiration is a motivating force in our writing group.

Appreciation goes to everyone in our weekly writing group for their pithy comments and helpful ideas as I worked on this writing endeavor. A big thank you goes to friends and family for their positive support and faith in me as a writer. For all of you, I am grateful.

A special thank you goes to Raul Villalva for his helpful ideas, support, and firsthand knowledge of the areas of Mexico mentioned in this novel.

Credits

Rain quotes from:
www.Brainyquote.com/topics/rain-quotes
www.quote fancy.com/rain quotes

Map:
www.North America-PICRYL Public Domain Image

Author photo by:
Juanita Martus

Author's Note

Personal Travel as Resource

My personal travels have taken me to many places, but for the intentions of this novel, some were helpful as resources for the story. I have toured numerous locations in Mexico, and among those mentioned in the narrative, the cities of Puebla and Cholula. I found the countless churches and enormous cathedrals staggering, and have attempted, in this story, to portray them as the historical icons that they are. I ascended to the summit of the pyramid in Cholula, encountering the view in the distance of the mountain peaks of Popocatepetl and Iztaccihuatl.

In the city of Puebla, a former Spanish colony, I toured the downtown area and observed colonial historic buildings such as the city hall area and stunning cathedral.

I journeyed to South Padre Island, Texas, primarily to witness the butterfly migration in October, and to participate in the annual Monarch Butterfly Festival held at the South Padre Island Birding and Nature Center. All of these experiences supplemented the creation of this novel.

www.ingramcontent.com/pod-product-compliance
Lightning Source LLC
LaVergne TN
LVHW041938070526
838199LV00051BA/2831